Original Bliss

Original Bliss

A. L. Kennedy

ALFRED A. KNOPF   NEW YORK   1999

Originally published (with ten short stories) in Great Britain
in 1997 by Jonathan Cape, London.

Library of Congress Cataloging-in-Publication Data
Kennedy, A. L.
Original bliss / A. L. Kennedy. — 1st American ed.
p.   cm.
ISBN 0-375-40272-1 (alk. paper)
I. Title.
PR6061.E5952075   1999
823'.914—dc21   98-15887
CIP

Manufactured in the United States of America
First American Edition

In memory of
Joseph Henry Price
1916–1996

Original Bliss

Mrs. Brindle lay on her living-room floor, watching her ceiling billow and blink with the cold, cold colours and the shadows of British Broadcast light. A presumably educative conversation washed across her and she was much too tired to sleep or listen, but that was okay, that was really quite all right.

"What about the etiquette of masturbation? Because everything runs to rules, you know, even the bad old sin of Onan. So what are the rules in this case? About whom may we masturbate?

"Someone we have only ever seen and never met?

"Quite common, almost a norm—we feel we are offending no one, we superimpose a personality on a picture, in as far as our dreadful needs must when that particular devil drives, and that's that."

Harold Wilson's baby, friend to the lonely, the Open University.

"How about a casual acquaintance? Someone with whom we have never been intimate and with whom we never will? Someone our attentions would only ever shock?

"Actually, that's much more rare. We imagine their, shall we say disgust, and find it inhibits us. We steer our thoughts another way."

Mrs. Brindle rolled onto her stomach, noticing vaguely how stiffened and tender her muscles had grown. Women of her age were not intended to rest on floors. Beside her head, the moving picture of a man with too much hair grinned clear across the screen. Video recorders were catching his every detail in who could tell how many homes where students and other interested parties were now sensibly unconscious in their beds, their learning postponed to coincide with convenience. Mrs. Brindle didn't care about education, she cared about company. She was here and almost watching, almost listening, because she could not be asleep. Other people studied at their leisure and worked towards degrees, Mrs. Brindle avoided the presence of night.

"On the other hand, we are highly likely to make imaginary use," the voice was soft, jovially clandestine, deep in the way that speech heard under water might be, "of someone with whom we intend to be intimate."

She tried to concentrate.

"The closer the two of us get, the more acceptable our fantasies become, until they grow up into facts and instead of the dreams that kept us company, we have memories—to say nothing of a real live partner with whom we may have decided to be in love.

"And here is where we reach my point, because this is all one huge demonstration of how the mind affects reality and reality affects the mind. I indulge in a spot of libidinous mental cartooning and what happens? A very demonstrable physical result. Not to mention a monumental slew of moral and emotional dilemmas, all of which may very well feed back to those realities I first drew upon to stimulate my mind, and around and around and around we go and where we'll stop, we do not know.

"That around and around is what I mean by Cybernetics. Don't believe a soul who tells you different—particularly if they're engineers. *This* is Cybernetics—literally, it means nothing more than steering. The way I steer me, the way you steer you. From the inside. Our interior lives have seismic effects on our exterior world. We have to wake up and think about that if we want to be really alive."

Something about the man was becoming persistent. Mrs. Brindle felt herself approach the slope of a blackout, the final acceleration into nowhere she needed to worry about, a well of extinguished responsibilities. It seemed not unlikely that his voice might follow her in.

She counted herself down the list of things still undone through her own deliberate fault: breakfast not prepared for, low milk not replaced, her surrender to the pointlessness inherent in ironing socks.

Original Bliss

. . .

Dawn was up before her, but still not entirely established, just a touch delicate. The television was dark and dumb in the corner. She must have remembered to turn it off. Her left hip throbbed alive, commemorating another night spent bearing her weight against a less than forgiving carpet. Not for the first time, she pushed herself up to her knees with thoughts of how much more convenient she might find a padded cell. The idea didn't crack a smile, not this morning.

Furious, humid rain was banging at the windows. Its noise must have roused her. She relished downpours, their atmosphere of release. Stepping gently through to the kitchen, she knew this particular pleasure came mainly from the air pressure falls that could accompany lavish rain. The harmless impacts of water on glass were among the small, domesticated sounds that Mrs. Brindle loved. Like the first whispers from a kettle when it clears its throat before a boil, they made her feel at home and peaceful in ways that many other things did not.

She steeped real coffee in the miniature cafetière that held exactly enough for one and tried not to remember the space in her morning routine. Mrs. Brindle tried not to think, "This is when you would have prayed. This is when you would have started your day by knowing the shape of your life."

While she sat and waited for the time when she could set the bacon to the grill, Mrs. Brindle remembered the programme she'd slept with last night. It had been about steering. A long-boned man who spoke about steering and wanking. That didn't seem exactly likely, now she thought, but the man who'd spoken seemed too coherent and unfamiliar and just too *tall* to be someone her imagination had simply conjured up and slipped inside her sleep. She hadn't exactly dreamed about him, but something of him had been constantly there, like the ticking of a clock, leaked in from another room.

Having completed her coffee, she worked her way through yesterday's paper and considered she might even try to find out his name.

"Edward E. Gluck. Edward E. Gluck. Edward E. Gluck. You hear that? I have a wonderfully rhythmical name. My mother gave it me. She played semi-professional oboe when she was young and I think this meant that she always approached things as if they were some kind of score: arguments, gas bills, christenings; anything. I could be wrong on this, but I like to believe it anyway, you know?"

Radio Two, Mrs. Brindle's favourite; it didn't pretend to be better than it was. She was mixing a batter for Yorkshire pudding, properly in advance so that it would settle and mature and make something which would taste well and be sympathetic with gravy. She was nowhere near the time for gravy yet.

As Edward E. Gluck repeated and repeated his own name, she recognised his voice. On the television, he had sounded just the same—he made very ordinary words seem dark and close. Now, beneath his enthusiasm, she could hear a harder type of consistent energy, unidentifiable, but engaging. She put the batter bowl into the fridge and sat to concentrate on Gluck.

"She was a lady, my mother. A remarkable woman. On the night I'm referring to, I was maybe four years old and unable to sleep because freight trains ran close by the back of our flat almost continuously. And I was restless because my parents had separated not long before and I'd been moved from my home and money was tight and sleeping seemed too much like dropping my guard. Anything could have happened while I was out.

"Now I remember this clearly. I'm sitting up, right inside the dark with the blankets neat in to my waist and the rest of me cold. I'm concentrating. But there's no way to know what I'm concentrating *on*—I only know I've *been* thinking when my mother opens up my door. She snaps me back from a place in my mind that is smooth and big and nowhere I've been before. I've liked it. I want to go there again, to the place that's only thoughts and me thinking them.

"Mother, she sat by my bed. I can still picture her

beautiful shape and know she smelt all powdery and breakable and sweet. She waited with me for the next of the trains to pass. She made me listen to the carriages—*listen* to them, not just hear.

"And they were saying my name. All of them, all of the time, for all of their journeys, were saying my name. *Edward E. Gluck, Edward E. Gluck, Edward E. Gluck*. Every train on every railway in the world can't help saying my name.

"That night, my mother taught me two things I have never forgotten since. That she loved me enough to offer me her time. And that my fundamental egomania will always cheer me up. I indulge it as often as I can."

Gluck talked a great deal about himself—he put his inside on his outside with a kind of clinical delight. Mrs. Brindle rolled cubes of pork in egg yolk and then salt and black pepper and flour and listened to someone with ridiculous personal confidence and a small but happy laugh. Whatever his life was doing, he seemed to understand it perfectly, because that was his job, his Cybernetics. Within the few minutes of his talk, he ricocheted from essential freedom to creative individuality and his new collection of accessible and entertaining essays which dealt with these and many other subjects. Available in larger bookshops now.

Mrs. Brindle knew about bookshops. For a while she had thought they might help her. Publishers were, after all, always bringing out books intended as guides to life and all-purpose inspirations. She had scoured an exhaustive number of first- and second-hand suppliers without finding a single volume of any use. She had also discovered since, that the fungi which thrived upon elderly books—even of the self-improving type—could cause hallucinations and psychosis and were, in short, a genuine threat to mental health. This did not surprise her.

The amount of time and hope she must have wasted in that particular search for enlightenment threatened to make her feel discontented now, so she decided to focus her mind on Gluck. She would like to read Gluck. This would do no more harm or good than the reading of anything else and would allow someone entertaining inside her head.

Her previous experiences had taught her that she could reach the closest sizeable bookshop, buy herself a book, and be home again in time to preserve the success of her evening meal. So she left the kitchen and then entirely abandoned the house with the radio still singing and murmuring to itself behind the locked front door.

She hadn't forgotten where to go. Through the side entrance and downstairs for RELIGION, SELF-HELP and PSYCHOLOGY. Those three sections always seemed to cling together, perhaps for mutual support. She was familiar with many of the titles they still displayed.

She was equally familiar with sidling across the broad face of SELF-HELP in the hope that she would appear to be very much on the way to somewhere else—perhaps towards HELPING OTHERS, or GENERAL FICTION—and not a person in need of assistance from any source. SELF-HELP was, in itself, an unhelpful title—Mrs. Brindle was unable to help herself, that was why she had bought so many books and found them so unsatisfactory. Their titles winked out at her now like the business cards of cheerful, alphabetical frauds.

Today, as always, there were no sections assigned to FEAR OF DYING, or ABSOLUTE LOSS. This was presumably due to a lack of demand. Or else the low spending power of readers overly obsessed with The Beyond.

Gluck's essays were piled on a table to one side of PSYCHOLOGY—twenty or so copies of a cream-coloured hardback with the author's name and title marked in hard, red type. She could also make out the cream image of a cleanly opened skull, still cradling the hemispheres of a brain, very slightly embossed. Lifting one copy, she ran her forefinger quietly over the curves and edges of the paper skull. It felt good. She allowed herself a pause. Finally, she split the fresh pages, smelt the bitterness of new print and gave the opening a skim.

For many decades an unholy alliance of neuro-physiologists and engineers has sought to produce mechanical imitations of the human brain.

In a few limited areas, they have succeeded. One might wonder why they persist in their attempts, when two sexually compatible and fertile human beings can develop the real McCoy and the perfect system for its support in a matter of months and at relatively little cost.

On the back of the dust-jacket there was a grainy photograph of Gluck—unsmiling and against a background of dramatic cloud. She could only see his head and shoulders, so it was impossible to tell if he was standing on a roof, or a cliff-top, or, indeed, the upper deck of an empty bus. Something about the light on his face suggested he had taken up a stance in front of a very large window. Perhaps he could afford a house where such things were available.

Meanwhile computerised technology has become increasingly sophisticated. We have witnessed the irresistible rise of successive generations of machines which add one to one to one, at ever more stupefying speeds. The computer has simultaneously come to represent, not an imitation of the human mind, but an emotionless goal to which it might, one day, aspire.

Half a dozen stops on the underground and she would be walking back home and no one need ever know she had run away. The book was a small thing, it could be put in a great many places. Not hidden, only put in a place that was safe.

Tunnel lights and stations roared and arched around her while she held *Gluck—The New Cybernetics* gently and privately against her coat. The firmness of the book's construction was reassuring and that was pleasant in itself; she shouldn't build up expectations for its contents. She should just occupy a little of her time with Professor Gluck's writing and maybe not actually understand a word, but that wouldn't matter. A dose of mild confusion would be nice, it wouldn't hurt. And she would be reading someone who really did know the mind: his own and other people's. He understood things and she could be there in his book while he was understanding.

As the train shivered and shook her, Mrs. Brindle recalled how much she had once looked for that, for understanding. She'd never wanted spirit guides, or dietary healing, aura manipulation, or the chance to be woken up sexually. She'd never wished to be a qualified stranger's second guess. She had never sought the temporary comfort of childhood hymns, of absolution, or even of very lovely Mysteries. Mrs. Brindle had only wanted someone who understood, a person who would tell her what was wrong and how to right it.

Somewhere in our science the original and the template have become confused. The limited, mechanical model is now used to analyse and find fault with the shamefully underexplored, biochemical original. The computer's admirable ability to store information and its rather more plodding efforts to draw conclusions from available facts are held up as the pinnacle of possible intelligence. Lack of flexibility and, above all, lack of emotional content in the storage and retrieval of information are regarded as essential. Already, in certain spheres, Reality and the hideously impoverished Virtual Reality are held to be completely interchangeable.

Political and social theories pursued on the basis of Numerical rather than Completed Facts, cannot be influenced by human joys or human pains. Is, for example, a death only a negative number in our combat readiness or population totals? Or is it a major intellectual and emotional loss? How will our species prosper if we treat ourselves, according to Numerical Facts, as no more than arithmetic? Humanity, its potential and inherent strengths as expressed in the human brain, are being systematically erased.

The New Cybernetics represents an effort to reverse this erasure. The following essays deal with its applications in the treatment of disease, information technology, the development of personality, learning and—more speculatively—in the fields of history, philosophy and ethics.

That night she re-ironed the collars and cuffs on four-teen shirts and then sat on the carpet with a black-and-white movie splaying out across the shadows of the room while she read Gluck.

At first she was afraid. She didn't want him to tell out every part of Mrs. Brindle into emptiness. Some things, she hoped, could never be wholly explained: how she laughed, the way she peeled oranges like her mother, what made her upset. She didn't want to learn that all of her was only atoms joining other atoms and cells joining cells and charges balancing up and down a wiring system that happened to bleed. Otherwise, all she'd have left of herself would be a type of biochemical legerdemain. She was afraid that Gluck might have the power to slip her apart and break her in the space left between nothing and nothing more.

But Gluck reassured. He wound her slowly through the glistening darkness she began to imagine was her mind. He personally assured her that she was *the miracle which makes itself.*

This was a start, a nice thing to know, but rather lonely. Before, Something Else had made her and looked upon her and seen that she was good.

Somewhere within her ten thousand million cells of thinking, she remembered when loneliness had been only an easily remedied misunderstanding of nature, because there had always been Something Else there, just out of reach. He had, at times, been more or less revealed, but had been always, absolutely, perpetually *there*: God. Her God. Infinitely accessible and a comfort in her flesh, He'd been her best kind of love. He'd willingly been a companion, a parent, a friend and He'd given her something she discovered other people rarely had: an utterly confident soul. Because Mrs. Brindle had never known an unanswered prayer. For decades, she had knelt and closed her eyes and then felt her head turn in to lean against the hot Heart of it all. The Heart had given round her, given her everything, lifted her, rocked her, drawn off unease and left her beautiful. Mrs. Brindle had been beautiful with faultless regularity.

Now she was no more than a bundle of preoccupations. She avoided the onset of despair with motiveless shopping and cleaning, improving her grasp of good cuisine and abandoning any trust in Self-Help books.

She had been told that her life in its current form represented normality. Existence in the real world was both repetitive and meaningless; these facts were absolute, no one could change them. Ecstasy was neither usual nor useful because of its tendency to distract, or even to produce dependency. Her original bliss had meant she was unbalanced, but now she had the chance to be steady and properly well.

Mrs. Brindle tried to seem contented in her suddenly normal life and to be adaptable for her new world, no matter how hard and cold this made every part of every thing she touched. She allowed herself to betray what she had lost by ceasing to long for it. But when her betrayal became too unbearable and she began to believe she was fatally alone, she tried to pray again.

At first her efforts felt like respectably articulated thought. No more than that. She found she had lost the power of reaching out. Now and again she could force up what felt like a shout, but then know it had fallen back against her face. Finally the phrases she attempted dwindled until they were only a background mumbling mashed in with the timeless times she had asked for help.

So Mrs. Brindle withdrew for consolation into the patterns of her day. She sought out small fulfilments actively. There were check-out assistants to be smiled for, chance encounters with cultivated or random flowers and overheard melodies to appreciate and, every week, she would do her utmost to find at least one new and stimulating, low-cost recipe. It was all bloody and bloody and then more bloody again, but faultlessly polite and inoffensive and there were no other bloody options she could take, but in her case, the path of least resistance was the one that she most wanted to resist.

Now another bloody year was grinding its way into June with hardly a protest or a sign of life.

Mrs. Brindle encouraged habit to initiate and regulate her movements in the absence of her interest and will. Friday morning's habit was the recipe trawl: twice round the local newsagents with a fall-back position provided by the library.

On the third Friday of June Mrs. Brindle found what she needed at only her second high-street stop. A belligerently cheerful magazine winked out at her, shamelessly covered with posing and pouting fruit flans: almond paste, cherries, apricots, vanilla cream and appropriate liqueurs; each of their possible elements boded well. She could explore a good dessert theme for weeks. This would be today's encouraging victory of the positive.

When she saw the article, the magazine's other article, the article which was not about transformative accessories, or any kind of flan, she was standing by her sink, holding a new cup of tea and half-looking out at signs of neglect in the window box. Somewhere beneath her breastbone she felt the warmth, not of surprise, but of familiarity and she may even have smiled down at the photograph of the prominent and fast becoming really rather fashionable Professor Edward E. Gluck. A small article mentioned his theories, his controversial Process and its undeniable results and she knew about these things already and in much more detail from his book. She was able to cast a knowing eye across the journalistic summary of his ideas and find it wanting. They didn't understand him the way she did.

Equally, they knew something she did not. They

were able to point out that Gluck would soon attend a meeting of high-powered minds in Germany. Professor Gluck would be resident in Stuttgart for at least the week that ran from one plainly given date in July up to another.

It seemed right that Mrs. Brindle should know where Gluck would be for the whole of one summer week. It seemed right that she should think of Gluck and Stuttgart and be happy and happiness is a considerable thing, a person should never underestimate what a person might do for it. Foreign travel might be seen as no more than a necessary inconvenience along the way. No matter how much justification and expenditure a trip—perhaps to Germany—would demand, it might seem possible, reasonable, worth it.

Having read Gluck as thoroughly as she could, Mrs. Brindle knew about obsession, its causes and signs. She was well equipped to consider whether she was currently obsessing over Gluck.

Certainly she was close to his mind, which might cause her to assume other kinds of proximity. Obsessive behaviour would read almost any meaning into even the most random collision of objects and incidents. Chance could be mistaken for Providence. Fortunately, her Self-Help reading meant that she knew her thinking very well and could be sure she was a person most unlikely to obsess. She had never intended to seek out Gluck, she had simply kept turning on through her life and finding he was there.

Original Bliss

· · ·

"Were you ever happy? Tell me, were you ever truly happy, that you can recall? The right-now, red-flesh and bone-marrow variety of happy—yards and yards of it? Hm?"

He had a tan. Professor Gluck was standing and talking like a real live person, right over there and with a tan.

And there was so much of him. Every shift of his shoulders, every weight change at his hips, gave her three dimensions of unnerving reality. She had guessed he was photogenic, that he made conscious efforts to shine, but she had not anticipated how very well-presented he might actually be.

"Happy so there's nothing to do except smile and smile and smile and then again, well, you could always smile."

Professor Gluck smiled luminously down about himself, as if to demonstrate. His little audience seemed to flinch gently, perhaps distressed by so much personality, all at once.

"Oh, the first time or two, you'll try to cough it up and maybe you'll shake your head about it, but in the end you'll just have to grit your teeth and grin it out. This is an inescapable thing you're dealing with. If you want to be happy—for example—it is highly likely that you will. The Process works. Naturally one can't infallibly predict the minutiae of its results, but speaking very strictly from my own experience I can say you may end up so contented you frighten strangers. Hold that thought. Now . . ." He paused and looked directly across to fix on Mrs. Brindle and she realised how completely she must appear to be out of her place. With only one glance he could tell who she was—the crazy woman who had written to him and said she would be on her way. "I am about to be late for an appointment. Thank you all."

The circle around him found its hands shaken and its shoulders patted aside as Gluck sleeked his way precisely to meet her. His attention withdrawn, the group shuffled and broke away.

"Mrs. um, Brindle?"

Something in her letter had persuaded him to meet her, which was good because it had taken her weeks to write. Her problem now would be that she couldn't make herself that clear again; not out loud where he could hear her. She was also too nervous to breathe. The uneasiness under her skin made her hands twitch while she tried not to gulp for air. She wanted to start this all over again at another, better time when she could feel more ready and less like a recently landed and naturally aquatic form of life.

Gluck's voice was unmistakable, dipping now and then into an octave below the norm, and holding that constant dry rumble beneath the rhythm of the words, his personal melody. "Mrs. Brindle. I am right?" His face waited, appraising.

He was said to be quite a singer. She had done her research. God, it was not fair or reasonable that she should be this afraid.

"Mrs. Brindle?"

"Yes, yes, you're right. Professor Gluck."

"My favourite sentence. 'You're right, Professor Gluck.' Well done. There's a table over by the wall where no one will bother us and I have asked for coffee, although it may well never come. Are you staying here?"

She felt herself propelled by something very like his will, or the sheer force of his words, or maybe just his hand, lightly settled at her back. She made a kind of answer without thinking, while her throat panicked tight. "Me? No. No, I'm not."

"Wise choice—I think this is the worst hotel I've never paid for." He nodded in passing at a young man with a briefcase, flapped his hand to a couple by the door, then inclined his head very slightly towards hers. "We may have to make a run for the last few yards, I feel the pack is closing fast." His mouth barely avoided a smile. "Oh, don't mind me, Mrs. Brindle—I've had to be charming all morning and it never agrees with me."

She didn't know if she minded him or not. She wasn't sure about the charming part, either, but he was undoubtedly something, a very great deal of something that was definitely Gluck. She walked on as carefully as she could, her awareness of his shape beside her threatening to distract her so much that she would fall. His hand continued to propel her with a useful and disinterested force.

Safely installed in their corner, Gluck lounged one leg out over the armrest of his chair, allowing it to be clear that he was both remarkably long-limbed and indisputably at ease with his surroundings. He seemed delighted that he might be adding creases to a suit, already expensively distressed. Now and then he spired his fingers, or bit his brown thumbs with his white incisors while he watched and grinned and watched, his interest held flawlessly at shoulder height. Once he had seen his fill beyond her, he angled round again to catch Mrs. Brindle whole and finish with one slow blink dropping down over eyes the colour of blue milk.

"Now we shall get to know each other, shan't we? But do relax first, it will save so much time."

She had already eased herself back in her seat and now tried not to move her arms in case they proved unreliable. Her limbs felt slightly less anxious now, but also strangely insubstantial. Still, it did seem she could trust both her hands not to shake. That was good, she could build on that. She just wished she didn't know she was pale and that there were obvious shadows around her eyes. Red was prickling on her cheeks and nose after yesterday's unaccustomed sun and she felt visibly sticky, despite the extremely efficient air conditioning at work on every side. Her physical condition should have been irrelevant—Gluck would hardly be concerned with how she looked—but she did wish she could have seemed slightly less hideous, for the sake of her pride. A person was unlikely to enjoy asking favours from a position of grotesque inferiority.

"Tchick, tchick, fffop. Zippo." Gluck winked at her and indicated a bullish man in his shirt sleeves who was straining at a fresh cigar. "Zippo lighters, they always sound the same. When I was younger, I wanted to smoke, just so I could use one." The white of his eyes blared a little too loudly over his grin.

"You never considered pyromania? Better for your health."

He sat round to stare at her squarely, his face shining briefly with a peculiar kind of appetite. "That's certainly true, certainly true. Remind me of what I can do for you, Mrs. Brindle. Now that we're really speaking."

She liked that she could sometimes change how people thought of her, just by saying out some little surprise. This didn't work in crowds because quite often no one heard her—she seemed often to be an inaudible person—but undoubtedly the good professor was now offering her a further chance to shine. He was trying to work her out, hoping to uncover just exactly who she was. She came very close to admitting she knew how he felt.

Gluck leaned in. "Don't be alarmed, by the way, if

we never get our coffee. They used to send it over with a very attractive young waitress—now she no longer comes and I often get nothing. You're in bad company with me, I do admit that, but I also wonder what precisely I did wrong. It is a shame, she was a nice girl."

She knew he was watching for a reaction, to check which offence she would take, and she tried to maintain a correct indifference. He drove on with his stare, unconvinced, and then exhaled into a kind of shrug. "Ah, well. I don't have your letter here with me . . . but . . . might I say first of all how impressed I am that you should have travelled so far. I do hope your journey will be adequately rewarded."

"I needed a holiday."

"And this is almost as good a location as any. Quite true. Do talk to me, Mrs. Brindle, I'm beginning to feel alone." Gluck pulled away, his eyes leaving first, cooling, their light closing down.

"You know about the brain. You . . . when you write—"

"I know about me, thank you. Tell me about you and your problem and I don't intend to rush you, but I must be in the Conference Room by 2:25 at the latest. You're attending the lectures?"

"Yes, I am."

"All of them?"

"Yes. Most of them, at least. Some aren't open to the public."

"So it isn't only my work that interests you?"

"Your work interests me the most. That's why I'm here. Please, if your time is so limited . . ."

She gathered a stiff breath and forced out something she hoped might be what she believed she thought, or hoped she thought, or hoped *he* thought, or just something *someone* might have thought at some time when they were trying to make sense of something. "Religious experience, spiritual feelings . . . do you know if it's only chemistry . . . electrical spasms. Can you tell if . . . ? Is it likely . . . anything . . . from descriptions. Do you know *that* process? Possibly it never occurred to you—why should it . . . I mean . . ." She tried not to sigh. "I have a problem."

"Obviously. One you currently seem quite unable to describe. Have you had a religious experience?"

"No, at least that's—"

"Would you like a religious experience?" He failed to hide the glint of a smirk.

"Spiritual."

"You would like a spiritual experience, or you would like a definition of a spiritual experience?"

"Either."

"I think you might be a little more specific about your requests—it's the only way to get what you want."

"I'm sorry." But she didn't feel sorry. Humiliated, that's what she felt.

"I certainly can't give you a spiritual experience."

Gluck's eyes were enjoying her unease, raising an unpleasant shine. He had decided to treat her as an interlude, a joke, and she wanted to be angry about that, but there was no room in her mind now to do anything but listen for what he might say. She was too hungry for any trace of help to be dignified. Their gazes crossed and locked and broke. Gluck's voice almost disappeared in a resonant rumble. "As far as definitions go . . . I could give you a roomful—chemistry, electricity, extremity, psychosis, psychotropics, trauma . . . If that all seems distressingly un-supernatural then you must simply remember that an answer is only true until it's been discredited. I don't work in a field of absolutes. Even a Completed Fact isn't really complete, it's just our current best attempt—a healthy admission of constant defeat. Sometimes a definition is no more than a convincingly detailed guess. Or are we talking about God? Faith? About which I know little or nothing."

"I'm sorry, I'm wasting your time. But there was something about your work, your understanding . . . there was a quality about it, perhaps not the theories themselves, but perhaps *in* the theories . . ."

The foyer, she knew, was quietly noting their every exchange: gestures, pauses, glances. She was using up time they wanted, wasting away the moments they could spend near their favourite: hoping for a trophy, a token, a moment of recognised intimacy; anxious to figure, even badly, in one of his famous anecdotes. If

Gluck himself registered their attention, he was keeping it tightly at bay.

"A quality. A spiritual quality in my theories? Hhum, well, that's natural—any genuine exploration will touch the boundaries of our experience, will press forward into what is unknown and possibly unknowable and there we will experience humility. Humility is, I believe, something somewhat on the spiritual side."

"You're humble? Even when you say you're an egomaniac?"

He licked away a sudden grin. "Remember when you quote from interviews, that they are very often works of fiction and should be treated as such. But yes, I am possessed of a considerable ego. I use the word in a strictly un-Freudian sense, no need to drag *him* in. But I still experience humility. I personally can be completely in awe of myself—humbled. I am, after all, working at the forefront of a field I single-handedly created. Good trick if you can do it." She watched as his face paused, relaxed, betrayed that it was frighteningly tired. "Mrs. Brindle, the size of the work and the beauty of it—not my part in it, the work itself—that is something humbling." He stopped again and might almost have sighed while he swept back a droop of his over-long hair. "I'm not helping you, am I? I can tell."

"What do you mean?"

"I mean, you are now frowning far more than when we first met and looking truly distressed. And we've had no coffee—I couldn't even offer you that. I have failed and, I'll be perfectly honest with you, I am no longer used to failing."

"No, I suppose not." She tried not to sound impatient. "Look, I didn't mean to . . . I think it's being here, this bloody foyer and all the people. I'm too tired now. And this heat is killing me. It was so hard to arrange a meeting and the hotel people here wasted so much time and I thought . . . I know you're leaving tomorrow and . . . Do you think I could speak to you? . . . later?" She dwindled to a quizzical whine and felt stupidly close to crying.

Gluck's head dipped forward, his voice emerging in a low, solid growl, unpleasantly patient. "Mrs. Brindle, as we speak, I am being considered for a Nobel Prize. Again. My lectures this week are relayed from the theatre to a hall that will barely accommodate my audience overspill. I have only recently declined the offer of an interview with a major—if mildly sleazy—gentleman's magazine. To be blunt, there are quite a few people, besides yourself, who would like to speak to me."

With her head lowered, he wouldn't notice that her eyes were closed, sealing in any sign of unsuitable emotion. "I quite understand. As I said, I came for a holiday. Thank you for . . . for your time."

He was standing over her, frowning her down, almost before she could reach for her bag.

"Mrs. Brindle, don't be so impulsive. You really are

a one for that, aren't you? All the way to Stuttgart with no guarantees . . . of any kind. No stopping you, is there, hn? It would be impossible for me to talk to *everyone*. That's what the lectures are for. But outside the lectures, I choose who I *like*."

His face cleared into a portrait of benevolence and she tried not to think of what he might mean and who he might like and how she might like to reach up and shake him by the shoulders so that Gluck could understand she was relying on what he could do to set her right.

He slowly sat and faced her and Mrs. Brindle thought she could see a change: a large, cool stillness in his eyes. Inside the mechanism, the metal, oil and cordite Gluck exercised each day—a little to butter his toast with, a little to light the world—he had decided about her.

"Could you tell me my position, Professor. I have to say, I think I'll miss your lecture. I'm sorry, but I need to sleep. I haven't been sleeping."

Gluck hunched his shoulders and pocketed his hands. This seemed to be a sign of real concentration, if not actual doubt.

"Professor? Your audience is waiting."

"Mm?"

"I don't think there's one person in this foyer who isn't watching us."

"No. There is one, if you check, by the windows. Her name is Frink . . . no, Frisch and she doesn't like me for reasons which are quite unscientific. I think we might be kind and summarise them as disappointment." Gluck took care to appear both modest and bemused. "She hasn't looked at me once all week which is some trick. Takes a lot of arranging. Anyway, what I was thinking was: there's an Italian place opposite the cathedral which you can't miss. Even when you're tired." A note in his voice cleared and his eyes dodged away. "You do, I beg your pardon, look tired. Go and get untired and . . . the best time would be about seven. Tonight. I'll be early, so you needn't bother. You look the early type. Is that all right." One straight glance, as if he was fixing her now for later use. "Mrs. Brindle?"

"Well. Yes. My hotel is . . . I'm not far from there."

"Fine." He was already standing, coughing, changing himself into something public. "That's fine then. We can shake hands now. Oh, and don't tell anyone." He smiled oddly. "If you don't want my audience, that is. Now, what looks like *goodbye forever*? Oh yes, I know." He pressed her hand lightly between both of his, the touch warm but dry. Although she was almost accustomed to something of his scent, his sudden approach left her breathing a pleasant mixture of soap, fabric, lotion. He smelt clean and mild and probably expensive with only the faintest undertaste of sweat. "And what about a Germanic bow?"

"I don't—"

"Customs of the country."

"You have . . . too much hair. I mean, I mean, I didn't mean to . . . mean anything. It would flop. That's all." She scrambled to smile intelligently while sounding entirely inane. Gluck remained unreadable.

"Well, in that case, I'll just have to leave. Seven o'clock. Ta ta."

He turned away and moved through the foyer with a kind of studied grace, head and slightly tensed shoulders above the general height.

In her hotel room, Mrs. Brindle went to bed. There she lay perfectly still and listened to American Forces Radio while it happily sang the praises of the wily Confederate J. G. Rains who invented fine bombs and lovely torpedoes and that all-time family favourite, the anti-personnel device—*another first for the American Civil War*. She listened to AP Network News. She listened to the excellent prospects awaiting in the US Postal Service for all those choosing to leave the Military. Finally she listened to the daytime murmur of the hotel surrounding her and the super-heated, orderly silence of Stuttgart beyond. She couldn't sleep for the ache of listening, her ears wouldn't fill.

The bath was clean and deep, if slightly too short to lie down in. The complimentary foaming body gel was not unpleasant; nor, for all it could matter, was the complimentary sewing kit. The towels were in good condition, neither overly soft nor harsh.

Clean carpet.

Bedsheet fresh and white.

She settled back beneath the quilt.

This wasn't going to work.

Mrs. Brindle's skin, even under the covers, felt impossibly naked—the touch of herself, alone with herself, the brush of her arm on her stomach, of her legs against her legs, tugged her awake. There was something unnatural about her. She felt her limbs cold. The sky that raked between the flimsy curtains was screaming with heat above ninety degrees and her room seemed hardly cooler, but she knew she had a shiver in her blood and whenever she lay down it showed.

The Konigsplatz was bending under the sun while a courteous electronic billboard noted the doggedly blistering temperature in degrees Celsius. She sat downwind of a fountain, trying to concentrate on its regular drifts of spray and the heat that lifted each droplet back up from her skin, almost before it fell. She was still tired and perhaps Gluck had only been joking, perhaps he wouldn't come. It would only be reasonable for him not to come—she was not famous and he was.

Mrs. Brindle knew she was wearing the wrong things, lifeless things, their colours insubstantial in the merciless light. A scrabble of panic touched her and faded again, leaving an airless tension in her chest. Gluck was making her frightened already, even though he wouldn't come. She would go to the restaurant and wait for him stupidly until she was too embarrassed not to go away.

Or he would come and then she would be too stupid with fear to make any sense and she would waste all the time she was going to get with him.

But that wouldn't happen, because he wouldn't come.

Beyond the flying water were parapets and cliffs of concrete. The whole city was boxed and canyoned in searing concrete and palely mountainous heat. British bombing had left only tiny islands of the past to stand: a church here, a municipal building there. The evidence of violence didn't disturb her, only the lack of a tangible past. She felt she had been lost in one vast, white amnesia.

"Amnesia?" Gluck's really very large hands killed another breadstick. The table that filled the space between them seemed strangely insufficient. Gluck was of a size to be invasive, effortlessly. "You're only abroad, Mrs. Brindle. That's not so bad, people do it all the time—it's called going on holiday."

"Well, I know that." She failed to sound anything other than abrupt.

"But even so?"

"But, even so, I didn't expect that when I left my country, everything else would leave me. I mean, if the people and the buildings are different—the churches—then I seem to stop believing in anything. I don't even believe in me."

"You are very tired, remember."

"Professor, it really isn't because I'm tired." He might be an expert on most things, but he wasn't an expert on her. "This started years ago, in Scotland, and now it's finished here. I am a person who has no faith. I'm over. That's that." Mrs. Brindle was the only expert on Mrs. Brindle that she knew. As a field of study she was more than specialised.

Gluck softly shook his head and rubbed at his fringe with one hand. A little shower of stubble fell to the tablecloth. For a moment, she couldn't think why and then she noticed. "You've cut your hair."

"Yes. About five hours ago. I've just spent most of one of them with you." He was trying to seem aggrieved and managing very well.

"All right. I didn't pay attention. I'm sorry. But I came here to talk to you seriously and I've now stared at three different courses that I couldn't eat because I have no appetite and because . . . because, to be honest, I'm nervous—"

"You don't say."

She thought of giving him a cold look, but then couldn't. He smiled gently and then she couldn't look at him at all. "Yes, okay. I know that you know that.

But all that we've done for one hour is discuss all the people you don't like at the conference and your favourite type of car and *nothing*. Now you want to discuss your hair?"

"I had it cut."

"I know you had it cut, that's why it's shorter."

"You didn't like the way it was, so I had it cut."

This made no sense. Gluck sat, his head seeming slightly larger, more plainly capable of holding all that thinking and more obviously grey. She wanted to be extremely angry with him, but nothing was coming out right and Gluck was being oddly tentative, tense. She could think of nothing to say but the truth.

"Professor, I don't know what's going on here."

"Nothing too out of the way, I assure you. I wanted to do something that would be pleasing, make you relax. Something like that." He coughed his way into a mumble. "Obviously I haven't been successful. But that's what I was trying to do. Small talk. And that kind of thing. I don't do it very often—work too much." Another, more forceful clearing of the throat. "Actually, it's the same with my hair. I usually cut it at home in my mirror to save time. The way it is doesn't bother me—I don't have to look at it, after all. So I get it damp, sellotape it down around my face—to keep it even—cut it a bit. Suits me. Suited me."

"That's nonsense." Still, it was drawing her in, however nonsensically.

"No it's not." Gluck registered a mild degree of

hurt. "That's how I do it. And I liked it long because I knew I was going grey, as you can see; or white. I thought of trimming back my sideburns where they're white." He turned his head to show her and rasp at one with his thumb. "But that could go on forever; I'd end up with a kind of bridle path cut over the top of my head and I wouldn't like that. I am vain."

He might have been stating his nationality, rather than a character defect. Gluck's vanity was part of Gluck and therefore could not be a fault.

"Professor, you don't need to talk to me, or to make me relax." A moment of irritation or alarm seemed to shadow across his eyes, but she continued anyway. "I don't relax any more. I don't expect to. Just tell me, can you help?"

He tapped at his glass and watched the red surface of the wine sway and settle. "I don't know."

She'd tried to be prepared in case he gave a sore answer, but what he said still hurt. Within the plainness of it, there was nowhere to fix a hope. He seemed to understand she needed more and went on.

"I would *like* to know. And to help. Very much. I feel for you. But I do not know. And now it's time for us to leave." He patted his jacket to find his wallet out and looked about him for their waiter; Edward E. Gluck, someone used to restaurants and being served.

Mrs. Brindle studied her dessert fork and tried to understand that this was all the time she would be given, finished and over with. She would have to go back to the dark in her hotel room and the night that was already waiting for her outside. Gluck had made her used to the pressure of his mind, his presence. It wasn't fair that he should make her so alone now and so fast.

"No—"

"Mrs. Brindle?"

She fumbled towards what she could tell him, now that she'd started to speak, and a broad, familiar sadness smeared all her words away. Why bother?

But to make him understand—only to try and make him understand—she lifted one of his hands—brown, healthy, heavy, warm—and pressed his fingers to the open face of her wrist. Her pulse overwhelmed itself while he held it, running dark and high with only her skin between him and her fear.

Gluck winced, but kept his hold. "What's the matter? What's wrong?" His voice smaller, close. "Mrs. Brindle?"

"That's the way it is. You feel that?" His face said that he did. "I'm scared. That's what's wrong. That's what's always wrong. I'm scared."

He smoothed his grip forward to cup her hand, whole inside his, and keep it as if she might be pulled away suddenly, against both their wills.

"Mrs. Brindle, there's no reason to be scared. Nothing will happen to you. We're leaving because I'm taking you somewhere else—a place where I'll be able to think and you can be distracted. Nothing bad will happen. Do you understand that."

"Of course not."

"Listen." The waiter hovered, courteously embarrassed by the way they were clutched together. "You say you've lost everything. Well then, how much worse can it get?"

Gluck passed over his credit card, while setting his focus firmly on her face. The waiter stalked away. "We are here now, in this moment, and nothing is anything other than it should be. We are both equipped with minds to perceive and alter all possible worlds—we will be fine."

She wouldn't have thought Gluck would be good at reassurance, but as he led her away to a taxi she felt something approaching safe. Mrs. Brindle did not wish to feel safe because of Gluck the man—she found that intellectually alarming—she would have preferred to find comfort in his thinking, his advice. Then again, any help should be appreciated and if she was feeling relief, it was her feeling so she would have it and like it, no matter who or what was responsible.

Gluck sat away from her in the back seat of the car, folded uneasily into the possible space. "This won't be a long journey. So we needn't talk. Unless you would like to. What do you think?"

Mrs. Brindle would have preferred not to think. Thinking at night was unsafe.

Original Bliss

He reached over and found her wrist faultlessly, no doubt in the evaluation of his touch. "You're not so frightened now."

It wasn't as if he was actually *holding* her hand. If he'd been *holding* her hand, she would have told him to stop. This was taking her pulse which was different, scientific. Still, she felt the uneasy snag of something: a cautionary chill tugging her back.

Gluck continued, touching, talking, "Not that I can tell anything except that your heart's going slower. I'm glad I'm not that kind of doctor." He released her back to herself.

"You don't like touching people?"

"Oh, I don't think that would be true, no. I just would have been no good—diagnosing and all that. So tell me how you are and then I won't have to guess." The bars and splashes of light from the windows made him seem to advance and retreat arbitrarily. "Mrs. Brindle?"

"It doesn't go away, the feeling, it only goes to sleep, so I can't. That's how I think about it. As soon as I'm not doing something, as soon as it gets dark, the thing wakes up and gets me. It always knows where I am."

"But what is the thing that wakes up?"

"Did anyone you cared about ever leave you?"

"Yes." He answered immediately, as if she had a perfect right to know. "My mother. She died while I was in America studying. I was twenty-two. We'd never been more than a few hours apart until that autumn. Not to bore you; she had looked after me before her divorce. My father didn't . . . I was too tall for him to like me. I stood out, annoyed him, made him want to knock me down. And she saved me. Always. When they separated she worked very hard and was very ashamed of herself so that I could be very educated and she could be very proud of me—from a suitable distance, of course.

"Blood clot on the brain. Killed her."

"I'm sorry." That sounded completely inadequate, even though it was true.

"Sorry? Oh, yes, so was I, but people adjust. Who did you lose?"

"God."

"Not a person?" He didn't understand.

But she might make him. "More than a person. Someone that was Everything, *in* everything. There wasn't a piece of the world that I could touch and not find Him inside it. All created things—I could see, I could smell that they'd *been* created. I could taste where He'd touched. He was that size of love. Can you imagine what might happen if a love so large simply left you for no reason you ever knew. One morning, you're looking through the window and you can't make any sense of the sky. It's like dying. Except it can't be, because dying ends up being what you want, but haven't got."

That was such a melodramatic thing to say, she

hoped he could tell it was only a fact now and something she was used to—not some kind of female, hysterical threat.

Instead of making any comment, he reached for where her hand rested on the seat and pushed his knuckles against hers with a light, slightly varying pressure that could not cause offence. They were driven on together quietly.

"Mrs. Brindle?" She had been letting her fingers relax against his so that their contact would not mean more than it should inadvertently. "Mrs. Brindle, I would rather not keep on calling you Mrs. Brindle. I would be quite happy to be Edward. Would you be happy to be something else? Something other than Mrs. Brindle?"

"Helen."

"Is that your name?"

"No, I just made it up. Of course it's my name. Helen. I've always been Helen."

"Not always Mrs. Brindle, though?"

"My maiden name was Howard. Helen Howard. Too many H's, really, for one person."

"So there was a Mr. Brindle?"

"There still is."

"Oh."

Helen realised she hadn't thought to mention Mr. Brindle before, because she hadn't thought of him, not for several days. She had forgotten him and never felt the difference. Astonishing. "He's at home. Didn't want to come. But, yes, he is at home."

"Why doesn't he . . ."

"Why doesn't he what?"

Gluck rubbed at the back of her hand and drew away, aligning his balance with a turn in the road. He set his fingers near his mouth and she realised without intending to that he was breathing in the scent of her skin from his hand while he thought of whatever it was that he couldn't quite say.

"What? Why doesn't he what?"

"It's none of my business."

"That doesn't matter."

"Well . . . I don't mean to presume, but I'm surprised he doesn't help you with this . . . your problem. Does he try? Does he know you're so upset?"

"Not all the time. There's no reason why he should. Not if I don't want him to. He's, um . . . he works, he's busy, and he's not, I don't know . . . religious. He didn't like it when I was. But the way I am—my problem—isn't his fault. This isn't his fault." She did think she was being accurate to say that—she wasn't defending him.

"Still, maybe it would be better if you were more alike." Gluck coughed, rubbed his neck.

"Maybe. But we're not. There's no point in thinking otherwise."

Inside the car, around them, Helen was sure she

could smell or feel a trace of Mr. Brindle: something at the edge of acrid and much too familiar.

"That's a shame."

"No, it's not." Helen knew she shouldn't let Gluck know this. "That's not a shame. I'll tell you what's a shame . . . But it'll sound stupid."

"I'm sure not."

"It is stupid. It's the most stupid thing I've ever known, but it's how I feel, it's how I've always felt.

"I can't stand his hair. Not the hair on his head—all his hair. He has so much hair. It doesn't stop. From the back of his skull and right the way down on his neck it stays thick, in fact it gets thicker and then it curls up into wool, black wool. I can feel it under his shirt, springy, as if he was already wearing something else. When he sweats, it stays with him. I imagine it running and sticking on him and then he doesn't seem clean. I don't think Mr. Brindle is clean. When he showers, the water kind of combs the hair out flat, but then it looks worse; like fur. Animals have fur. People don't have fur. Well, do they?"

"I . . . some men . . . I don't . . . have fur. Only the usual. Not that it's . . . relevant. Not fur, no."

"It makes me panic sometimes when he wants to touch me." Edward had turned to his window, away from her. "I don't mind that, though. The first time I ever had . . . had a sexual . . . I mean, fear seems to be good for me, for that kind of thing. It can make you more aware—because of the adrenalin, I suppose. I'm sorry, this has nothing to do with anything." Her breathing felt light-headed, strange.

"I would have thought it was to do with you."

"Yes, but if I was working correctly I wouldn't mind about him. He would be my husband and that would be all right."

"I see. I think I see. We're here, by the way."

Helen realised the car had stopped.

As they walked into what appeared to be an ageing warehouse, Edward moved around her, near but never touching, opening doors and clearing a path through the orderly crowd inside. He was keeping her insulated. She couldn't tell who was in need of protection and who was being dangerous, but began to step tight in beside Gluck, as if she might indeed be incorrectly wired in some way and pose a potential risk.

The tiny auditorium filled and manoeuvred beyond her while she let herself be eased in ahead of Gluck. Somewhere a smoke machine began to spit and bluster enthusiastically.

"Now." Edward sidled close between the rows of seats and put himself next to her. She was reminded again that public spaces seemed never to be designed for men of his proportions.

"What is this?"

"Nothing at the moment." Gluck smiled quickly, then stopped himself. "But it *will* be modern dance. It always helps me think. I have no idea why and not the vaguest desire to find out. I go with the flow and watch. After I met you, I booked the seats."

"Modern dance."

"It's just what we need now, trust me. They're from Finland, apparently."

"Finnish modern dance."

"It'll be a distraction. And it really will help my mind to clear. I use it a lot. How are you feeling? Be specific."

"I—" She took a moment to check. "All right. I feel all right."

"Good. You see, people *don't* feel bad constantly. Not always. They simply don't bother to monitor how they are with any accuracy. When we're un-selfconscious, we actually get relief. But we don't notice or remember, because it happens when we're not being conscious of ourselves."

A heavy chord of electronic sound beat up through their long bones and their chairs and jarred at the gathering smoke.

Edward inclined towards her knowledgeably, "Ah, that'll be us starting, then. The music is usually a clue." He fed his legs forward under the seat ahead of him and let his chin slump to his chest. Helen watched while a huddle of slender young women circled each other out from the wings and stood. They shuddered as a mass. Then stood. The smoke banked and thickened round them. A man in the front row began to cough.

For thirty-eight minutes, Helen was aware of the movement in Edward's breath and careful not to answer the rhythm of pressure where their shoulders couldn't help but meet as they sat. Synthesised music shuddered her ribs, or screamed in her teeth and the seven women twitched towards and away from each other across the stage. The obscuring influence of the smoke became a blessing, albeit mixed. Helen couldn't tell if Edward was enjoying this. She only knew he was trying not to choke on the chemical mist.

Green lights arced through the fog as one and then another and then all of the dancers tugged at the lengths of muslin which had been keeping them more or less wrapped. The cue for their closing blackout was apparently the unveiling of the final pair of breasts. Helen felt a crawl in the skin beside her jaw. She didn't mind the nudity, it was hardly offensive. She minded that half-naked women were happening now, while Edward was here. They made her position seem odd.

"Come on now, interval." Edward sneezed. "Excuse me. That smoke." And then grinned.

Helen waited, surrounded by closed German conversation, while Edward slipped his way back from the bar. Naturally, his height gave him a clear view across the room to her. He was trying to catch her eye, but she couldn't let him.

"There you are."

She gripped the damp of the glass, avoiding his hand. "Thanks. So this is the interval, then."

"Yes. But another two sections to go . . ." He laughed suddenly, as if someone had shoved the sound through him. His head tilted back and to the side and he unsteadied his feet in a kind of private confusion that seemed peculiarly young. "Oh, I am sorry. You can't stand it, can you?"

"Well—"

"Of course, you can't. Because it was total crap: so bad it was almost hypnotic. That's what I love about bad dance, it's utterly, utterly meaningless and wonderful to think against." He was checking her face to see how upset she was, trying to say what she would agree with, trying too hard. "And there we had a perfect example. Not one redeeming feature. Bad music, bad dancing and, Jesus Christ, bad smoke."

"But on interesting themes."

"Hm?" She'd made him puzzled. She'd made him stop.

"Themes—constipation and electrocution. That's what it looked like, anyway." He bent into another sudden yelp. She'd made him laugh. She liked him laughing. "From Finland? Seven dancers?"

"Mm." He wiped his eyes.

"You know what that would make them?" The last word came out as a squawk, but she couldn't laugh yet because that would stop her speaking.

"What?"

"The Seven Deadly Finns."

Edward wheezed and then whimpered while he shook his head and she couldn't help doing much the same. He patted her shoulder and buckled again. The other dance connoisseurs edged away from them, unimpressed.

Edward took a long moment to lean on her arm. "That's dreadful. That is the worst thing I've heard in years. Oh God, I can't breathe." He smothered a giggle. "Can I take it we won't be going inside for instalments two and three."

"Not unless you want me to swallow my own arms in despair."

"Dear me, no. And maybe they'd make us look at more breasts. That was too many breasts."

Her answer was overly fast, "Only the usual number."

"What, two each? Yes, but fourteen, all together and with bandages . . . I'm not used to that." He pondered the floor. "They didn't . . ."

"Bother me? No. Not at all."

"Good. I wouldn't have liked them to."

Once the warehouse bar had emptied, they found seats and Edward bought her another drink.

"Only soda water, this time."

"Yes, I quite understand." He squinted down at her contentedly. "Don't want to get carried away. Clear head." And, having turned away, "Nice to see you laughing."

"Hm?"

"I won't be a minute. You take a seat."

When he came to sit beside her in the still of the room, free from obstacles or constrictions, he began to take his own scale again. His movements became more fluid, graceful.

"Do you know how tall I am, Helen?"

"No. I suppose, really quite tall . . ."

"Quite. Six foot three-and-three-quarter inches. Observers may not be clear on the detail—those extra three quarters—but I'm not exactly a secret I can keep. Helen, I can change my mind, I can turn the inside of myself into absolutely anything. I've taken Quantum Field Theory—the maps it makes for the universe and matter and time—and I've turned it back in to chart the brain that thought it. I've taught myself how to know the answer and let the question find itself. I've made me a genius. But I can't be any smaller than I am. It used to annoy the hell out of me."

"You look good tall."

"Haven't got much choice, have I? Thanks, though." He rubbed at his neck. "And I'm used to it now. At school I was taller than my teachers, I stood out in crowds at my universities. I stood out. Jesus, I *had* to be a genius so people wouldn't go on about my height. And you know what I actually wanted? Hm?"

"No."

"To be good."

"Good?"

"Well, don't sound quite so surprised—it could have been possible. At one point. I wanted to be a good man—the way that James Stewart was good. You know—James Stewart? I think I've seen most of the films that he made, maybe all. Even the one with Lassie.

"Nobody ever noticed he was tall and skinny. They didn't look down Main Street after Destry rode again and say, 'Bloody hell, he's a bit tall, isn't he? Spidery. Clumsy, too.' No, they all said, 'What a nice man.' 'What a good man.' Because he was.

"People loved Jimmy. *I* did. I *do*. Like when he's George Bailey in *It's A Wonderful Life*? Good old George. And *aaaw, the good old Building and Loan.*" He let out an impressively recognisable crackling drawl, then couldn't help a grin.

"That's the only impression I do—practised it for years. That character Bailey, you stick with him, like you do all the time with Jimmy. You want the best things to happen to him, nothing but happiness. When he's down, you stay with him because he might need company and when he's up again you're glad to see it because he makes you feel generous and you believe he *could* have a guardian angel to keep him from suicide and perhaps it'll notice you. Jimmy's special."

Edward beamed, unashamed.

"You stay with him in that story to the end and it's all good—even the badness is good. Even when he makes mistakes, they're good mistakes and he can mend them.

"I do tend to wonder—if I'm not careful—just how well I would measure up if my guardian angel delivered me into one of Jimmy's lives. I'm pretty sure I wouldn't come off well. I'm not good—only tall."

He was fishing for a compliment, so Helen thought he might as well get one. "You've been good to me."

Edward shook his head solemnly, "Doesn't count."

"Why not?"

"Because I wanted to."

She nudged his forearm and found that she was grinning and frowning without those actions being contradictory. "All right then, your work does good. When people use the Process, they needn't be hospitalised all the time, or drugged. You let people be happy. And you refused to work for the army."

"You've been doing your research."

"Only now and then."

"That's okay, they can't touch you for it." He allowed himself a strange, quiet smile. "And you're right, I couldn't work for the army. But then nobody sane ever could. My God, you can't imagine what they wanted me to do. I mean, they would have loved our Finnish friends—deafening noise, chemical smoke, a sealed white box full of threatening figures—just the thing to soften you up before they ask your life away.

"Seriously—they would try anything. Because they do understand that the enemy they most have to conquer is in between their ears. We all face the same puzzle with that—except that some of us are explorers and some of us are bombers and some of us are speculators on property we do not own."

"You explore."

"Yes. But not because I'm good—just because it's the loveliest thing to do."

Their hands were already loose amongst the glasses on the table-top, it was very easy for them to find each other and fasten, hand over hand over hand over hand while Helen felt a rattle of alarm, like a stick drawn fast along a hard fence. Very far away, her Old Love was observing. Her Maker. She watched her fingers, pale and small in comparison to Edward's.

"Edward, I don't mean anything by this. It's only reall—"

He was nodding before she could finish, "I know." He began to lift her hands, "I don't mean anything by it either." Steering her up and apart from their table to a point where they could stand, hands now in a knot between them. "Of course I don't."

Helen moved through her thinking and was almost certain that she was nothing but concentration and memory and the possession of an open, hopeful mind. He was a good man, despite what he said, and he would give her an answer and that would be all. First the trust to touch each other, that relaxation, and then the answer when she was sure to be listening. That made perfect sense.

"I mainly wanted to make it clear," he unfastened her hands, only to slip inside them and hold her by the shoulders, "that you are an extremely good person and in here," leaning forward now, cautiously, "in here," he kissed her forehead, with a moment's release of static energy. "In here, you have everything you need to get better. In this part of a part of a second, you have it all. That's reality, not wishful thinking.

"Not that I don't like . . ."

Helen, because of a small discomfort she had in her arms, an idea that things should be other than they were,

". . . wishful . . ."

pulled him in to rest against her,

". . . thinking."

A button of his shirt was at her cheek along with the slow heat of him. "In fact I like wishful thinking a lot. Hello, there." She could feel his voice, burrowing through him.

"Hello, sorry."

"Don't mention it. Are you scared again?"

"No. I don't think so." While her heart lunged against her, amoral and unlikely.

"Good."

When the audience straggled out from the auditorium again, she and Gluck stepped away from each other smartly and then stood, uneasy within their new distances. Helen thought they should speak, but they didn't.

In the dim interior rock of another cab, Helen was quite aware she was returning to her hotel, but she seemed able to face her arrival and the way time would then press on. The thought of her life, outside and waiting, was no longer impossible. She tried to imagine turning off the light in her room and letting the nothing fall into her head where it could hurt her, but she couldn't believe that as her future now.

Edward nudged her shoulder, "All right?"

"Mm hm."

"I've had a good evening, by the way. Thank you. I don't do this very much. Socialising."

"I would have thought you did it all the time."

"Then you would have thought wrong. Public faces for public places—not really me. As you might have noticed, I sometimes just want to be offensive when I've had too much handshaking stuff. It makes me grumpy. But of course, I'm such a hound for the limelight, I couldn't walk away and be private—I'd pine."

"That would be awful."

"Yes, I pine extremely badly." He coughed tidily and, when he raised his head again, was serious. "But that isn't what I want to talk about."

So now he would tell her, he would give her help. That would be fine, what she came for. All the way to Stuttgart and no stopping her, like he'd said. She would get what she came for and she would be fine.

She turned for his shape in the dark. "What *do* you want to talk about, then?"

She could feel the press of him looking, holding the look.

"What do you want? Edward?"

"Want? To say the things I already should have. I've spent all night, telling you nothing of any particular use. Partly to have your company . . ." He flinched his head a little. "But mainly because I don't know what to offer for the best. You should have the best—you're the kind of person who always should. Do remember that, won't you?"

"Okay."

"I don't have much I can tell you."

"That's all right." It was easy to listen in the dark without having to worry how her face might change as she heard what he had to say.

"When my mother died, I was over at UCLA. There was no warning and nothing meaningful that I could do. I flew back home and did my funeral duty for other people, but not for her. My father wasn't there—he'd committed suicide maybe seven years before. Had Parkinson's Disease and he couldn't face the way he'd go. Now I could have helped him with that. If I'd wanted to."

Helen hadn't heard that edge in his voice before.

"When I went back to the States, all my mourning performances done, there was no one there. No one for me. Before, no matter what happened—right or wrong—my mother was around. I didn't worry her for most of the time, but she was always a possibility of help. I could call her and not really talk about anything, only hear her being herself and that would be enough. I'd put down the phone, sure of what I should do.

"You have to remember, she was the woman who saved my life. Often. My father would have killed me, but he didn't. She got in his way. We both know about losing things, hm?"

As if her presence was part of his thinking, he didn't seem to expect an answer, but she spoke because he sounded lonely. "That's right."

"I'm not upsetting you?" His voice sharpened in concern.

"No. Unless you're upsetting yourself."

"No." He twisted slightly to face her through the dark. "For a long time after her death, I was numb; absent but functioning." Helen nodded without thinking—she knew about that one. "So I started to talk to my mother in my head. I began to live—far more than I had while she was with me—according to what I imagined might be her wishes. I have to say, we've parted company since. And it was my loss. But that way of thinking about her and getting myself through is still available to me and would still work, I'm sure."

"And you think I could do the same with God."

"You can't have faith if you need evidence. You used to have evidence—that's very unusual—God touching you. Now He doesn't do it. Perhaps that's about faith. Do you call your God *Him*?"

"Yes."

"*Her* would sound odd? *It*?"

"I know God's not a person, but *He* has always suited me."

"So you do still believe in something about Him. Start with that. Not that I know anything about this."

"You're making sense. And I will try."

"But don't sound like that." He caught at her elbow, then released her just as suddenly.

"Like what?"

"As if I've volunteered you to walk across hot coals. You're not on your own, you know."

"You're leaving tomorrow."

A little silence blundered between them after she said that, as if his absence drew in closer when they mentioned it. She wouldn't miss him, she hadn't known him long enough. He would be leaving her what he'd said, what she wanted; what she'd been looking for. Helen couldn't think how many years had passed now, since she'd last got what she'd looked for. Nobody could just step up and cure her, but he'd done his best and, in this field, Edward's best was the best there could be.

He stretched and then folded his arms. "Yes. Yes I am going tomorrow, but I'm not ceasing to exist."

"No, you're not." Helen was sounding ridiculously glum which was bad of her—Gluck was doing all he could.

"What do you want? Should I promise I'll write?" Now he sounded uncomfortable, which was her fault.

"You don't have my address."

"You put it on top of your letter. I'm a genius—I notice that kind of stuff. Listen . . ." She found her hand taking his, recognising the heat and depth of the fingers. "Mm hm, hello again." They both smiled, their mouths invisible. "Listen, I saw my mother hurt, physically, by someone else and that wasn't the worst thing. I couldn't bear the ways she hurt herself inside. Every year beyond the divorce, I'd see her cry while I opened my Christmas presents because, yes, she was happy about our being there together and safe—all of that—but she'd also convinced herself that anything she gave me wouldn't be enough. She wanted to be married for me and make a good family. She robbed herself of joy. All the time. Like he had."

Original Bliss

Edward nudged in beside her as his voice fell soft. "It wouldn't take a Jung or a Freud to work out that I'm never going to like a woman I respect and care for being in emotional pain. I'm going to want to help."

Helen listened to his breathing and tried to remember the way she would be at home and the proper order of her life. She shivered with a small belief in the disapproval of Something other than herself. Edward shouldn't write to her. It would be bad if he did: good, but bad. She loosed his fingers and rested her palms across her lap.

"You needn't write."

"I know I needn't. I don't need to do anything. I've worked for decades to reach the point where I can have that degree of choice. So I do what I want to and I want to write. Okay?"

"Okay. But there can't be . . . I should explain . . ."

The cab slowed into the pedestrian precinct where her hotel hid itself. The coloured illumination from silent shop-fronts swept them both.

"Ah, you see that?" Edward pressed to her side of the seat.

"What?"

"*Welt Der Erotik*. A chain of popular Bavarian sex shops. See them all over the place. I'm sorry, I'm changing the subject very badly because we're nearly home. For you. You didn't want to know about sex shops."

"I suppose I might have—"

"No. I think you might not. Is this where you are?"

"Oh." She recognised the entrance. "Yes. This is it. Let me—"

"No. You don't pay for anything. Because this way you've had a nice time and you haven't had to pay for it later. We've established that principle, which I think is good. I'm guessing you had a nice time, of course."

"Thank you. I did."

"Good." He spoke a few words of German to the driver, who turned his engine off. "Now, Mrs. Brindle, we don't have to make this look like *goodbye forever.*"

"But it will be *goodbye for a very long time.*"

"I should think that would look pretty much like forever, though, wouldn't you?"

"Then can I do something I want?"

Something fluttered in the air between them, rocked.

"Absolutely. Do your worst."

Helen did nothing bad, or worse, or worst. She rested a hand to his shoulder for balance and then executed motions that could be summarised as a kiss, the mildest relaxation of his lips leaving her with a sense of somewhere extraordinarily soft.

Edward scratched his throat thoughtfully. "Well. I was going to do something *I* wanted as well, but now I'd just be kissing you back and I hate to be repetitive. Thanks." He searched for something else to say and couldn't find it. "Good night." Eyes slightly taken aback by his ending so abruptly, he presented his hand, angled for shaking, and she accepted its weight.

"Yes. Good night. And goodbye for a very long time."

"That's right, but I won't say so, because I do dislike goodbyes. So. Good night."

They let each other go.

Helen walked herself across the hotel foyer and into the tight, brass lift with the porthole window that periscoped its way up to her floor and to her room and to her self.

Her self wasn't bad to be with tonight, not unpleasant company. She removed her sandals and her skirt, seeing how the heat and sitting had creased it and wondering when she'd begun to get so dishevelled: at the start of the evening, or later when it would have mattered less. Not that it actually mattered, either way.

She took off her blouse. Several available mirrors told her there was too much contrast between her usual colour and the places on her body she'd allowed to see the sun. She didn't look healthy, overall.

With a little more attention, she watched as she unfastened her bra. Her breasts were not like a dancer's, they lacked that kind of discipline, and they were larger. They had what she thought of as a better roundness. In spite of gravity. Probably not to everyone's taste, but then they didn't have to be.

The bra was nice, too—she supposed, a sort of favourite, if she had such a thing—swapped at Marks and Spencer's for one Mr. Brindle gave her on a birthday. He'd never noticed the change.

Her knickers were the ones she'd bought at the airport because the airport was where she'd remembered that she'd packed none of her own. If a person has been very tired for a very long time, she will tend to forget things like that—essential items.

When she was naked, the mirror stared back at her until she realised she was thinking of the Seven Deadly Finns and of laughing. The mirror smiled and then looked away. Surely to God she hadn't been smiling like that all evening? That wasn't how she'd meant to be. The mirror slipped back to its grin, it didn't mind.

In bed, she turned the light out and this wasn't a problem.

This wasn't a problem.

Somewhere, a door muttered closed, but there seemed to be nothing dreadful in the quiet between the building's minor sounds. There was nothing like death in the dark. Helen was not tempted to lie and listen to the buzz of blood round her brain and wait for something bad to go wrong. Tonight she did not think forever would come and tell her how large it could be and how quickly she would disappear inside it. Forever would not make her alone, it would just remind her of Edward and saying *goodbye forever* with him which was sad but not frightening. She was determined within herself that there would be no more harm in darkness, only sleep.

There was no harm in Edward, either; no harm in her choosing to not bath now, to not wash him away before she went to bed. Edward was an influence for good, because he wanted to be and because keeping a trace of him with her tonight was bringing her up against the force of Law. She was doing a little wrong, and finding Someone there who would object. A touch of her God was back. His disapproval set a charge in the air, a palpable gift.

Perhaps because of this, she tucked her thoughts in under her eyelids and discovered she had the security she needed to reach for sleep. She rolled close up in the dark, pulled it round her skin and, for one soft second, knew she was all underway, about to be snuffed like a lazy light.

Helen bumped and drifted down through a loosening awareness, before she stepped out and into a fully-formed dream. It was one she'd seen before, but not recently.

Above her was the high, grubby ceiling of her old school's Assembly Hall and everywhere was the sound of the tick of the loudest clock in the world. The invigilator paced. Helen had lifted her head and was resting inside the familiar discomfort of her school uniform—tight waistband, lots of black and blue.

She was sitting her Chemistry Higher, the final paper, the one with long answers that had to be written out. She'd chosen her questions, managed the topics, been finished in good time.

Fifteen minutes left. She was cautiously aware of other heads bowing, shaking, being scratched at with biro-ends.

Twelve minutes left and there was no more anxiety. This hadn't been so bad. She should just check things over now, take it easy and make sure she'd done her best. Her experimental drawings were lousy, but that shouldn't matter much: they would work and they were clear and she wasn't expected to be artistic, anyway.

Eight minutes left and it hit. A tangible, audible, battering terror that coiled and span and folded round and round itself down from her collarbone, to mesh cold through her body and then push an inside ache along her thighs. Eight minutes left.

She absolutely knew. She'd done it wrong. Helen had done it wrong. She was meant to check how many questions she should pick and get that absolutely right; it wasn't very difficult after all: it was printed at the top of the paper for anyone but an idiot to read and one too many answers was almost as bad as one too few, but she had one too few which was the worst. Everything had been fine—now it was the worst.

Original Bliss

During her dream, time condensed as it did when she had been, in wide-awake reality, sitting and feeling the sweat from her hands beginning to distort her papers. Trying to avoid any sign of flurry, or any irregularity of breath, she had searched for a question she could possibly answer in not enough time—something even halfway likely. Organic, possibly.

Even with so many years between her and the examination, even deep asleep, her mind could reproduce the horrible wordings of 14a, and 14b, through to 14e.

Part of her then had locked into problem-solving, while her hands had twitched themselves towards legibility. Part of her had been otherwise concerned. Five minutes left and the lick of fear inside her swam into place and fixed her flat to something she had never known before. With the fifth and final section of question 14 still undone, her eyes closed without her consent and the proper force of panic began to penetrate. Rolling smoothly in from the small of her back, she had the clearest sensation of rapid descent, of wonderful relaxation and then monumental tension holding in and reaching in and pressing in for something of her own that wasn't there, but would be soon.

Helen tried not to smile or frown. She steadied herself against an insistent pressure breaking out between her hips and sucking and diving and sucking and diving and sucking her fast away. Four minutes, three minutes, two. A shudder was visible at her jaw.

And then her breathing seemed much freer and she was perhaps warm, or actually hot, but oddly easy in her mind. She slipped in her final answer, just under the given time, before sitting back and watching the man who was her Chemistry teacher collect in what he needed from them all. She wondered briefly what he was like when he went back home beyond the school where both of them did the work they were expected to.

He was a man. She'd been told about men. Men had necessary orgasms which allowed them to ejaculate and have children. Women's orgasms, on the other hand, had been hinted around in Biology as a relatively pointless sexual extravagance.

Helen had very recently decided she was quite in favour of pointless sexual extravagance.

She'd felt strange walking out of the hall, secret, and barely curious about her marks for Chemistry.

Helen's night-time mind was able to observe while the door through which her younger self was leaving gently tipped and shivered and folded down into a small horizon, out of her way. She was alone in a sunlit space now, with something like a fountain for company and a figure far off, but walking towards her and holding yellow papers in his hand. Helen couldn't think why he seemed familiar—he had no tell-tale points to give a clue—still, she knew him. She recognised him in her sleep.

Helen twisted from her side on to her back, one

unconscious hand still resting near her waist. Her dream dipped closer, licked at her ear, hard and dark, and said, "Do not look at the man. Do not look at him unless you have to and sometimes you *will* have to because he will be there. Then you can look, but you must never for a moment think that you want to fuck him, to fuck him whole, to fuck him until all his bones are opened up and he can't think and you've loosened away his identity like rusty paint. Don't think you want to blaze right over him like sin. Don't think you want to fuck him and fuck him and then start up and fuck him all over again. Do not think about fucking him. Think of your intentions and he will see, because they will leak out in the colour of your eyes and what do you think will happen then?"

Helen, warm in her dream, began to smile and the man and the sunlight across him began to sink and slur away. Thinking of nothing at all, or nothing harmful, she moved towards a very pleasant rest.

"Mrs. Brindle? Helen? Hello?"

Her hand had reached for the telephone without the ring of it having fully woken her.

"Mrs. Brindle?"

"Uh, yes."

"You sound groggy, that's wonderful."

"Who is this?"

"Edward. Edward Gluck. You were asleep, weren't

you? And I thought you would be out by now and see-ing sights . . . I suppose Stuttgart does have sights—has anyone said? You've slept."

"Yes, I . . . Professor, Edward—I suppose I must have been asleep."

"Do you know what time it is?"

"Time?"

"The time of day. No, don't bother looking I'll tell you—two o'clock in the afternoon."

"What?"

"Two o'clock. Do you feel better? No, you won't be feeling anything, yet. Wonderful. You slept. I'm so glad, really I am. First time in a while, hm? Good. The reason I was calling: I thought we might discuss your diet." He seemed to be hurrying over a catalogue of topics he might wish to hit. "The timing of your meals and their composition; there isn't too much available about the dietary requirements of the Process in the public domain. I mean, you won't have read about it. So have lunch with me. How do you feel? Did I ask that?"

"I don't know. I don't—Is it really two o'clock?"

"Ten past the hour. You'll be hungry soon."

"You're leaving today. You don't have time."

"Always have time for your interests, Helen, you never know what they'll give you, if you let them have their head. I'll meet you by Reception at three, no three fifteen."

"Reception here?"

"Yes, Reception here. Your hotel. Three fifteen. You slept. Well done. Oh, and goodbye. Bye."

For some time, she kept the receiver by her head and listened to the tone on the line. When she felt sure that Edward's call had happened and that she was awake, she began to feel happy. Happy was the first emotion of her day and a person couldn't ask much more than that. She got up.

Helen stood in the bath and opened the shower, let it roll down her body, nicely cool and good to lift her arms in and turn underneath.

Past two o'clock in the afternoon; that meant she'd been out for more than twelve hours and she felt like it, too, extremely relaxed. She didn't dwell too deeply on her excursions into Stuttgart the night before, but she was glad to admit that the miniature Process she and Edward made together must have set to work. She had been right to come here and had been rewarded with sleep. She tried to think of something thankful she might say to God.

The clean flow of the shower washed her free of any after-taste her dreams could have been tempted to leave. Now she deserved a celebration with the man who had helped her begin to be put right.

Gluck was sitting at the side of the Reception desk, dressed down in blue jeans and a grey shirt. He was more obviously slim today and it occurred to Helen that he might well be quite physically fit, not only active in the brain. He unfolded himself upwards and offered his hand.

"Ah, Helen."

"Edward."

"Yes, Edward, you remembered." He said that in a way that made sure she could tell he was pleased to be Edward with her. Edward would be what he preferred, not Professor Gluck. "So, good afternoon. You look well. Terrific."

They went and ate beef with onion gravy and little noodles and extra bread and then something with hot cherries in and Helen was hungry for all of it. Edward observed her appetite and talked seriously, almost formally, about the chemical implications of his work. If he knew enough about her—purely factually—he could work out a programme of general nutrition and supplements that would definitely help her to at least feel more contented for more of the time.

"Are you suggesting anti-depressants?"

"Helen, do I look insane? You know my opinions on that. Those things don't make you happy. They just mean you can't remember you're depressed. Anyway, you're not depressed."

He looked at her for too long.

"Then what am I?"

"If it wouldn't make you sad to hear it, I think you're bereaved."

So that was it. Now she could understand how he

thought of her. That was good. His phone call, his attentiveness, new gentleness, his eagerness to offer her whatever came into his mind were all because she was God's widow and that deserved respect.

Helen was relieved, definitely mainly relieved. She could now accept Edward's kindness without reservation because what they were to each other had been made quite clear. This was all good, entirely good; in no way disappointing.

He strolled her back towards her hotel through a chain of pedestrian precincts and underpasses, not taking her arm when the crowds seemed to threaten, but somehow suggesting in his stance that he would be ready to do so, if required. Helen reassured him about her enjoyment of the heat, her lack of fatigue and the pleasantness of the lunch they'd shared. He submitted to each of her statements with a steady and caretaking smile.

Edward would go away after this and she would have another rest until the evening and perhaps some room-service sandwiches. He had seen her through the end of her crisis, apparently, and there would be no need for her to bother him any more. No need for her even to write. Today she could think there was mercy beyond her in a place she couldn't see and that her time would pass and she would be content. She would apply herself and look forward to that.

"Here we are, then, home."

Edward nodded and held the hotel door out wide for her while she stepped inside. He followed and she turned to him.

"That was . . . I do appreciate your letting me have such a lot of your time. When is your flight?"

He shifted his weight very gently towards one hip and glanced away. "I had to leave the Summit—enough is enough—and I did intend to leave Stuttgart, yes. Then I changed my mind."

"Why?" Having asked this, she found she didn't want to know.

"I'm not sure. I think I needed a rest. You'll know all about that. When I go back to London, I'll be rushing straight into something. The sooner I get there, the sooner it starts and I want another two or three days to be on my own."

"I'm sorry you've had to spend so long with me."

"Oh no, that was just like being alone." He flinched at himself. "I do apologise. That isn't at all what I meant." She let him pat at one of her shoulders. "I mean you were an absolute relief to be with. Very educated people—no—very educated *academics* are not always very intelligent and certainly not always good company." He shook his head in almost serious despair at himself. "And all of this only proves what I said before—James Stewart would have told you the *right* thing there: that you are intelligent and good company. Of course, *I* managed to mess it up."

"Oh, I don't know. From what I remember, James could be quite charmingly embarrassed. When he did mess up."

Edward looked out over her head and then let himself examine her, while she examined him. "Like I said—intelligent. I think I'd better get up to my room."

She let herself giggle. "No, wrong hotel. This is where *I* get up to *my* room."

"I didn't say? I'm staying here now."

"You're what?"

"Well, I could hardly claim to be leaving Stuttgart if I didn't even check out of my hotel." He was taking pains to sound plausible. "Now I'm in hiding. Will you give me away?"

"No. Of course not."

"Good."

They rode the lift together in silence, Helen thinking her way through a mainly numb surprise. Edward had chosen to stay here. He must have thought it might suit him—couldn't be bothered to try somewhere else. That must have been it. That made sense.

Edward's floor slid down around them and together they jolted into place. He nodded to himself as he set off away from her, inclining his head round to say, "Obviously, this isn't the last time we'll meet, but I won't impose. I have a lot here to keep me occupied. I promise." He seemed keen to be reassuring—she must have appeared more concerned than she wanted to.

"Goodbye, then, Edward."

He nodded to himself. "I hope not completely goodbye." The lift door began to glide shut. "But I definitely won't impose. See you."

She didn't reply, the lift having closed against her before she could usefully speak.

For two breakfasts, Helen approached the dining-room with a tick of anxiety in her chest. She couldn't be sure if he would be there, already picking through the buffet, or if he might emerge while she drank her coffee and gathered her concentration for the day. Nothing would be more normal, people tended to eat their breakfasts at breakfast time, and he would probably come to sit with her because that would be the civil thing to do, but early-morning conversation usually left her in a state of unconditional defeat. She didn't look forward to failing to impress.

As an exercise, she tried to imagine the way she ate breakfasts at home. At home; that other place. She made an effort to think of what happened there. Did Mr. Brindle ever compliment her bacon, ask her to pass the jam? Helen found it difficult to remember. There was also something mildly irrelevant about that house, that kitchen, that tired stumble through tea-making and toast and being sure to put the milk in the fridge and the bread in the bread bin and not the reverse, even if you are crying tired, because you don't want to excuse and explain yourself again; when the whole point to your situation is that it does not change and Mr. Brindle, you already know, hates explanations.

But now her situation *had* changed. Helen was falling faster and faster and faster asleep. She had unreasonable energy and appetite. When she flew back to Scotland, she wouldn't be able to stop herself looking different. Mr. Brindle might not like her different.

"My husband doesn't understand me."

She practically did say that out loud. As if the snugly breakfasting couples and tidy families would have the remotest interest in the way that her life had been melted down into an unconvincing sexual cliché.

Of course, she needn't have worried, not as far as being joined for breakfast went. Edward either didn't like food in the mornings, or ate it in his room. He was true to his word and did not impose. Edward neither purposely disturbed her nor crossed her path accidentally when she slipped out to visit the gallery, or to buy Mr. Brindle a present from the specialist hologram shop.

Helen was aware that if a person was expecting someone, even in an uneasy way, and that someone did not then arrive, a person might feel disappointed. That person might miss the opportunity of finding that someone inconvenient.

Added to which, Helen had a very good reason for

speaking to Edward again. She wanted to say how much better she was. She could not do anything but delight in walking for hours without feeling faint, or buying and eating two whole pretzels on impulse and then a slice of apple cake, because the food was there and she was there and she wanted to eat very much. When strangers looked at her, their eyes did not pause for an instant too long, clouding with concern or embarrassment. She was smiling out and other people were smiling in. If there was still only minor comfort from the world beyond this one, she was at least finding a compensation in things present and tangible. It would only be fair to thank Edward for his part in that.

By her third unattended breakfast, Helen began to wonder how long Gluck would be in Stuttgart. Maybe he'd already left and not told her. This seemed unlikely but not completely out of the way. More to the point, she was only staying for two more days herself. Then she would have to go home.

People went home all the time, it was something they liked to do, because home was a comfortable feeling and not just a building they'd lived in before. Helen knew this in theory, but not in experience.

"Edward?"

"Hello?" His voice was slightly cautious and faint along the line as she sat on her bed and wondered about the best things to say in the call.

"Edward?"

Now she could hear him being happy. "Oh. Hello. It's Helen, isn't it?" He was happy to hear her. "How nice. What day is it?"

"You mean you don't know?"

"That's precisely what I mean. When I'm very involved in something, I lose track." He sounded more preoccupied than brusque, but she was sorry she'd disturbed him.

"No, no. You haven't disturbed me. Thursday already . . . I wouldn't have guessed that. And you're leaving me when?"

"I'm leaving you—I'm leaving Stuttgart on Saturday morning."

"Then, if you'll forgive me, I won't suggest that I take you for dinner. There are things I have to finish with here." Helen felt a blunt disappointment nudging in. "But if you wouldn't mind, if you're not doing anything else, I would really appreciate if we had a drink together in the first-floor bar at something like nine. Or half past. That would do me a monstrous favour, actually." He was trying too hard again, being too studiously polite. "I need a break. And I want to say cheerio. And see how you are. Of course. How are you?"

"Well. Very. Nine would be good."

"That's splendid. I shall aim towards you then."

"Nine it is." As she spoke, the hot metal smell of prohibition breezed in about her—a signal that something of God might not be too far away, because even if He was a He, God disapproved of men. Helen had always been taught that, and told not to meddle with them.

But she didn't intend to meddle, so all she had to do was appreciate the clearer trace of Presence in her room.

"Helen, don't go."

His voice snatched her back to the receiver.

"I wasn't. What's the matter?"

"Well, no, there's nothing the matter. Do I sound as if there is?"

"A bit."

"Oh. No, I'm only tired. Don't worry. I . . . I wanted to thank you for calling. That's all. I needed this, really." He did sound tired. "One of the hazards of the Process, or of the powers it will release, is an increase in one's capacity to focus on an activity for very long periods. This can be extremely useful, but it can also be extremely like going to jail. I forget I own the pass key. Um, listen, my room is 307, could you knock on my door and come to get me? I'd hate to lose the place again. Help me with that, could you? Hm?"

So at a touch before nine o'clock—it does no harm to be prompt—Helen rode the lift to Edward's floor and walked along a hallway he must have been quite familiar with by now and reached his door and waited. She realised she had no ideas about what to do next.

"Edward? Edward."

She could hear movement and then a shout. "Hello. Yes."

"Well, should I knock, or should I tell you who it is?"

"Never called on a gentleman in his hotel room, hm?" The shout was nearer.

"No."

"I don't know if," a lock turned, "gentleman is exactly accurate . . ." and the door eased open. "Anyway, never mind knocking, just come in. Oh, yes, and maybe tell me who you are." His gaze slithered below her face.

"Me."

He shook his head slightly as if trying to clear his mind, offered her a nod, a grin. "Oh. Hello, me. Hello, you. Good. Good."

307 was not untidy, more like dishevelled. The furniture and fittings made a left-handed copy of her own room, two floors above, but there was a smell of human warmth here, not unpleasant but slightly unexpected, intimate. Edward, who was not dishevelled, more like untidy, waved her towards a seat as he struck out purposefully for the bathroom.

"I *am* ready and I *was* expecting you, all I need to do is shave. Obviously. Sorry. Sit down. Won't be long."

Sure enough, the abrasive buzz of an electric razor worried into life and Helen waited, glanced around. Edward's desk was mountainous with papers, articles, folders and what she assumed were his hand-written notes. In the same way she tended to look through other people's windows when they left them bared at night, Helen had never been able to resist the attractions of a working table-top.

She slipped over to stand above his papers while Edward continued shaving with what sounded like considerable force. This was where he worked—where he was a genius for real, pacing his mind against itself with no one ahead to stop him and no one behind him to fear.

While taps ran in the bathroom, she had enough time to scan diagrams in heavy black ink, sheets of dense typing and a stack of photographs. She could have examined all the pictures, but the first one stopped her. Initially, Helen tried to understand it and was pausing simply to do that, but then its meaning decoded completely in a rush and she stood and looked and stood and looked because the image wouldn't let her remember that she could do anything else.

The girl had shockingly white skin and made a remarkable background for her hair which shone, oil-black and long enough to rest on her shoulders. A dark stubble showed at her underarms and a fuller shadow glistened between her legs. Her mouth was pursed in something like concentration. Beneath the girl was a man, also stripped but almost hidden, and beneath him was a chair, hardly visible. The girl's weight seemed borne almost entirely on her braced calves and arched feet. There was visible tension in her thighs. Also there was the other thing: what they were doing.

After an indeterminate time, Helen stepped back and to the side and paused, avoiding an opinion of any kind. Gluck emerged: tie neat, cuffs buttoned, cheeks thoroughly cleaned and smoothed. The combination of fresh aftershave and laundered cloth made her think instantly of home and good evenings she could remember having a while ago. This was the scent of being close and then going out to move among strangers and get closer still. Edward smiled and she didn't join him.

When he asked her, they were in the lift. "You saw those photos, didn't you? On my desk."

"Yes. No. Only one." Her left side was against the safely carpeted wall, her right side towards him.

"I thought you had. I'm sorry they upset you. They are upsetting." He rubbed at one of his eyes. "I am . . . ahm . . . conducting research into paraphilia, Helen. And a group I advise is trying to treat men who have an addictive use of pornography. They are people who deserve our sympathy, our help."

"I'm sure."

"Don't say that, if you aren't going to mean it." He spoke softly without facing her.

"I'm sorry. I misunderstood."

"That's all right. Understandable."

The lift doors opened and she tried not to step out too fast. Edward hung back, eventually being forced on to the landing to save being shut back inside and dropped away. Then he stood and watched her until he seemed satisfied she would hear him out.

"I wouldn't have shocked you for anything. I'm sorry. I was too tired to think straight; I should have cleared the damn things away. They're not even necessary. But please understand, these people need help. We're not talking about recreational use—that kind of relaxation—whatever you happen to think of it. We're looking at a group of men who make themselves almost incapable of sustaining relationships with other human beings in the real world. If they ever have intimate partners, they can't cope. Their jobs come under threat, they lose interest in their surroundings, they don't eat, their lives are centred around a satisfaction they find harder and harder to achieve. De-conditioning can help them to an extent, but they need something better than that. I hope to find that better something." He rested his palms at both of her shoulders and let her study his face. "I am sorry. Please. Helen."

"Please what? I don't know what you're asking me for."

"Help me not to spoil our night."

As he dipped his head forward, she understood she should kiss his cheek and that made them fine again, sorted out.

Edward shut his eyes and released a breath. "Come into the bar and talk to me—so I don't think about all of that pain." He looked sad tonight and there was a hesitancy, a light hurt laid across the way he moved. "Will you do that?"

"Yes. I can do that. Anyway, I'll try."

Edward's third wheat beer was mostly done when Jimmy Stewart decided to put an appearance in. "*Aaaw, you know, I think we should drink a toast to good old Bailey Park.*" Edward was trying to please her, to joke her out of the stillness that fell whenever she thought of leaving Stuttgart and goodbyes. "*Whadaya think?*"

"Bailey Park? You'll have to tell me, I don't know it."

Genuinely amazed, Edward let Jimmy's drawl desert him. "Bailey Park. You really don't know? Don't remember? But you're such a clever woman with everything else."

She felt pleased out of all proportion, but muffled her smile.

"Everybody has blind spots. How are you at choux pastry?"

"Okay, you've got me there." He couldn't suppress a type of grin. "Pastry, though, I don't mean to . . . but I can't imagine you. You standing in a kitchen, making pastry."

"I did try standing in the garden, but the flour kept blowing away."

"Should have tried the flour bed, hm?" He sipped his drink, trying out an expression that she hadn't seen before. He was being careful until he could tell if she'd let him be daft. For the first time, she realised he was wary of what she might think.

"Go on, less of your nonsense."

He peered down at his feet, apparently on the verge of being happy. She tapped at his hand.

"Tell me about Bailey Park. Complete my education."

"Well, Bailey Park was the housing estate that George Bailey built in *It's A Wonderful Life*. People left their overpriced, rented slums—you never had to see them, you could imagine—and they went to live in the houses that George had built them with the money they'd invested in the good old Building and Loan. It was like a possible Promised Land. Good houses and good people, doing good things—the whole place made the way that George would like it. Good old George. So here's to Bailey Park."

"You want me to drink to a housing estate."

"Not *any* estate. *The* estate. All put together with dignity and love. George built it for people. How many things are really *for* people? Can I tell you a secret?"

There was no possible answer but yes.

"I mean it, I want to tell you a secret, Helen. So what you have to do is think if you should allow a man you don't know too well, a man in a bar in a foreign country, to confide in you." He watched his glass closely, as if it might run away.

"Confide away. It's nice to be confided in."

"You'll think I'm odd."

"I think you're a genius."

"That's very . . ." Gluck gulped at the last of his beer in lieu of finishing the sentence.

"What's your secret. I won't tell."

"Oh, I know that. Absolutely." He softened his voice and spoke as if he was describing a sleeping child. "It's only an idea, not really a secret. Once upon a time, I was trying to say what I wanted to open up within the brain. I could have said that I'd found a way to chart the Field of Thought and to evade both time and circumstance, and explore all the solutions of the world. I've uncovered what makes me. I am a leap of faith, I am a flight. To steal from the language of physics, I am a constant singularity—a perpetual process of massive change. You, too—naturally."

He lifted his gaze from the table. She didn't know how best to look back at him: an absolutely self-made man.

"I'd been asked to explain myself and the Process, yet again, and I'd even begun to reel off the usual guff when I stopped because something else made much more sense. To me, it made more sense. I wanted to say that our minds were made to give everyone the chance of Bailey Park. The place we take with us, wherever we go—the place that *is* us—we can build it

into Bailey Park, we can live in bliss. We have a chance
at it, anyway. I have found out a tiny amount about
how this can be and I call that the Process, but I know
I've hardly begun."

"Did you say that? About Bailey Park?"

"No. No, the man I was speaking to represented the
Pentagon. He wanted me to work within their
Advanced Research Projects Agency and—apart from
many other terrible things—he was keen that I should
teach young men and women how to do terrible
things terribly well and without thinking. They
wanted to take the pain from the records of war—no
more emotional memories, just objectives achieved,
rates of success. I don't think the Pentagon understands about Bailey Park. Or bliss."

"You didn't work for them."

"Of course I didn't. You know me; I couldn't have.
And I'm not an American. That made it easier to
refuse."

"Were they difficult?"

"Well, these NSA hit-men keep trying to shoot
me . . ."

"What?" She hadn't meant to sound worried, but it
happened anyway, even though he was obviously joking.

"No. I don't do work in America now, that's all.
Which is a shame, because I made some good friends
there. But Bailey Park, that's the place." He raised his
glass and she brought hers to meet it. His hand

wavered as he set it down. "I'm so tired. You know, I've just noticed. Tired, tired, tired."

So they talked nonsense about the Finnish dancers and gently enjoyed each other. Helen tried to frame what she wanted to say—a thorough goodbye and thank you.

"Edward?"

"Helen."

"I think, it really is time—"

"I know. I was trying to gather my thoughts for a half-way coherent farewell and I couldn't think of anything adequate. Tonight I'm no good."

"No, well, yes, there is that. Which is . . . it's hard, isn't it?"

"Yes. I would rather not start saying out loud how much I've enjoyed, well—you, basically. Us. If I mention that, I'm admitting we're about to stop."

"I know. But I want to say thank you. I mean I'm slee—"

His eyes snapped alight. "I know. You're sleeping. You're coming back to yourself."

"That's right. Ever since the night with the Finns. I did enjoy that."

"Except for not eating the meal and loathing the dancers and hating me."

"I didn't hate you."

"At the start."

"I possibly didn't like you very much."

They began to stand, preparing to finish the evening.

"But you do like me now?"

"Obviously." They walked carefully.

"Very much?" His words tried to be as weightless as they could—no pressure, no threat.

"I can't answer that."

"Why not?"

"It would go to your head." She paused and a beat later, he did, too. "Thank you for your help, Professor Gluck."

"Thank you for yours, Mrs. Brindle."

Instead of moving outside the bar and towards the lift, they stood for a little together, not speaking, Helen thinking about her full name and what it meant. Mrs. Brindle, married to Mr. Brindle and about to go home. Slowly, Helen became aware of a pale, metallic sensation in her limbs. Her face began to feel clumsy and unpredictable.

Edward cleared his throat. "Come on then."

Helen reached into her bag, fumbled for her door-key and picked it out, although she had no immediate need for it. They began to walk again.

Staring softly ahead, Edward waited for the lift to arrive and take them in. "This is horrible."

"Yes." She touched him on the arm, quite close to his shoulder. For perhaps the better part of one second, her palm and fingers rested against cloth and she felt him, she absolutely felt him, like a flash photograph taken in skin and expanding around her skull, around her mouth, around her waist and in. She felt him. Here was the curve and dip and warmness of his arm, the muscle and the mind moving lightly beneath his shirt. Here was the way he would look: the smoothness, the colour, the climb to his collarbone, the closeness of his torso and the speed of his blood. Here was the scent of the taste of him. He would taste good, because a good man would. Before she could finish her breath and lift her hand away again, she knew precisely how a kiss or a lick at his naked arm would taste. Good.

"That's us, then."

"Hm?" She watched the lift doors split apart. "Oh, yes."

And they rode up together. Two floors. Twelve seconds. Helen counted them.

"Goodbye, then."

Helen intended to tell him "goodbye" back, but he kissed her on the mouth, suddenly, dryly, and stopped her telling him anything. Then the doors began to move and he was moving too, leaving, gone.

In her room that night, Helen bathed and thought of nothing at all. She dried her body slowly and looked in her mirror and she kept on thinking of nothing at all.

At a touch past midnight, her phone rang. She knew who it would be.

"Edward?"

"Oh, you knew." There was a broad pause. "I'm sorry it's so late. I've just noticed." His tone seemed less substantial than usual.

"That's all right. Is something the matter? Edward? Is there something wrong?" She listened while he breathed quietly, but enough for her to hear. "Edward, what's wrong?"

"Oh, yes. I'm sorry. I shouldn't bother you. It's simply . . . I was looking through this material again and it makes me so depressed. It makes me so unhappy, Helen, to think of it."

"You mean those men? The photographs?"

"It's all so awful."

"Yes, but you're going to help them and you know the Process works. They'll be fine. It's normal to be disturbed by other people's pain."

"Yes, I suppose. Other people's. But it makes me feel lonely, you know? Something about it makes me lonely and I thought that calling you would help. It was a silly idea." His articulation sharpened. "I mean, speaking to you does make me feel less lonely, but it's silly of me to impose, to let this stuff get to me." He began to sound angry with himself. "I've seen worse. I should just say that I really did enjoy meeting you and that I would be very happy to receive a letter from you now and again. I would like to know how you're sleeping. Hm?"

Helen was growing more awake and able to appreciate his thinking of her—even if it was rather late. "I will write to you. I . . . do you need? . . . Edward, are you all right now? Is there anything I can do?" There were things she could offer him, naturally, but it was late and her suggestions might be inappropriate.

"I'm fine, really. I've been working too long on one thing, that's all. I'll wish you goodnight."

Helen didn't answer, knowing he intended to go on.

"Oh but, Helen, it's all such dreadful stuff. I apologise for talking about this, but it really is such dreadful stuff. If I *can't* talk about it, the things don't seem real. If I can't tell you . . . I look at this and the life it has seems . . . I don't know, *more* than mine."

She heard him change his grip on the receiver.

"I don't know why I'm doing this. I shouldn't, but I will."

His voice was nearer now.

"I am sorry, but, I have a picture here of a woman with two men inside her. That's what I'm looking at. A picture in a magazine. Her with the two men. Her lips don't really hide the first guy's shaft—the shaft of his prick, which is really quite a size. I'd guess she couldn't take it all in her throat, but this is her ideal position in any case, because these photographs are meant to help us understand the whole of her truth. We have to see the suck *and* the prick. *And* the fuck. Her second companion fucks her anally, of course, we can see most of him—the part that counts—as well as the lift of her arse, her willingness, openness. He's wearing dark-coloured socks, the second man, he has varicose veins—not bad, but noticeable.

"Have you ever seen two pricks in a woman, up close? I've got pictures of that, too—fucking the arse and the cunt?—it doesn't look like anything you could think of. The penises make one, fat kind of rope that greases and sews right through her. On video, they pulse in and out of time, like something feeding, a fuck's parasite.

"Helen, everything is so clear, far clearer than life. They're here for me to watch them, the two men shoving themselves into pleasure, and the woman having none. She's there to make them come, to make whoever's looking come; that's the entire reason for her, no need to add a single thing. The men can touch all of her, inside and out, but they needn't make her come, they needn't even use her cunt if they don't want to. She's just there to get it where it's put. No pleasure, no fun. Unless, of course, she can take solace from ejaculation for ejaculation's sake. If she does that, then she's a dirty bitch, a slut who deserves every bad thing she gets, even if that includes gang rape at the hands of her camera crew which I know will happen if I turn on a couple of pages, or so. I have looked at this booklet before. She will be used and humiliated by seven men while her mouth has the wrong emotions and her eyes shut down.

"Any sane and normal person would see her condition and wish only to be usefully compassionate. That's the way to be, Helen, that's the way to be. The Bailey Park way to be. Anybody good and with a heart would be afraid to imagine how she must feel. You can understand that, can't you. Helen?"

She was able to say yes.

"I am making sense. I know that. I'm not too drunk to make sense, only drunk enough to let me tell you this. Helen, listen to me. You should listen. Are you listening?"

"Yes." She can hear an uneasiness, a movement, shaking his breath.

"I want you to find me out . . . You would be bound to and I can't wait. Helen, the girl in this picture, I want to know how she feels. I want to know exactly how she feels.

"I want to know how she feels right up inside, when I'm up to my balls in her, my prick after all the other pricks, after what they've done. I want to have her, too. And she would want me, the pictures make her made that way. I want to be in her while she's raw, while she's open all the way to her fucking womb— and she is opened up, I can see it. I can see every-thing—the way she's full of it, running with it, her cunt and the other men's spunk. I want to be up her and make her full of me. I want to come. Helen, I want to come. I do. Then I want to see them having her again and we'll go turn and turn about her, turn and turn about her everywhere. Everywhere. I mean there isn't any end to what I want. There is no end, Helen.

"I can't bear the way I always turn out to be. I'm telling you, I'll never get out of this, I understand that. Sometimes I can manage containment, but that's all.

"I can't help you any more, Mrs. Brindle, I'm the wrong man for the job. I'm the wrong man. You'll get better—"

She knew she was going to hang up, but the sound of the receiver falling still gave her a kind of jolt. Gradually, she discovered that she felt very peaceful, not needing to do anything: to cry, to move, to remember the edge in his words and the heat. She would turn out the light now, to calm herself and dream. Decisions could be taken in the morning, if there were any to take. It seemed there might only be one and that it was taken.

At about two a.m., the phone rang. She counted to twenty before it stopped and the silence sucked in around her again with a hissing throb. The noise hadn't disturbed her, she hadn't been asleep.

Mr. Brindle didn't like his present much.

"What's this?"

Really she should have given it to him before dinner, because then the overbaking on the pie-crust wouldn't already have made him annoyed. It was strange how quickly she could drift out of practice with pastry and baking—a few days off and her presentation began to slip into collapse.

"What is it?"

"A hologram."

He was gripping the picture's frame with both hands, angling it forward and back, but staring at her so, of course, he couldn't be able to see the image change. "I know it's a hologram, I've seen them before. I mean what is it supposed to be. I can't see a thing."

"I'm sorry I went away."

"I'm not talking about that. I'm talking about this: your present to me which doesn't work. If I want to be

angry about your running off across Europe with your
lunatic sister and to hell with me, then I'll be angry
about that. I have free will. That's what you tell me,
isn't it?"

"Yes."

"Well?"

"I think it will work where there's more light."

"And?"

"She needed to get away." Mrs. Brindle com-
pounded her lie, her original lie, the one that would
follow her around now until she either forgot to feel
guilty or forgot the truth. And, then again, a lie com-
pounds itself if a person only lets it take its head. "The
divorce and everything—she needed a holiday." She
held her face calm, her eyes unwary and offered Mr.
Brindle a taste of her perfectly honest shame which he
could interpret as he liked: a response to her failed
obligation, hidden transgression, contemplated adul-
tery. God knew which.

"I'm not talking about your sister. I'm talking about
this. Not that there's any point. It isn't working."

Mr. Brindle set the picture down next to his
uncleared plate and gave her the chance to take both
her offences away. The hologram would have to be
disposed of with the bad pastry, but she hoped she
would have more luck with the summer pudding and
the lightly cinnamon-flavoured cream. Mr. Brindle
always enjoyed that and it looked wonderful to serve,
all the different colours of red, the new season's fruit

that made her kitchen smell of berry-picking and being much younger than now.

She sat back at the table and watched him tasting, examining, turning the white cream and the bleeding fruit together into something spoiled and pink. If she'd been sticking to the Process and its dietary advices, she couldn't have been eating this. Instead, she would have bought the supplements and trace elements suggested; the ones that were too numerous to be hidden successfully anywhere in Mr. Brindle's house.

Mr. Brindle began to eat steadily, contentment in a shine across his forehead and his lips. Mr. Brindle hadn't been angry about her trip yet, but probably he needn't be tonight. Later would do. When he handed her his bowl, he wasn't frowning. He even rubbed his index finger over the back of her hand.

Because she had been away and he might have thought about that, thought about her not being in any way available to him, he might ask her to be with him tonight. Not that they didn't share a bed usually, but he might have recalled the way they used to commemorate their sharing of occupancy. She wouldn't deny him. A refusal would be unwise and he wouldn't be demanding, not more than once. They would try to read each other, and then discover again they were written in two different languages, were quite untranslatable. Their intentions would subside, or rather, Mr. Brindle's intentions would subside. After an hour or so, she could leave him and come down-stairs to anticipate a morning made hopeful by the simplicity she planned into her daylight hours.

Her days at home after Stuttgart could seem so much like her days before that Mrs. Brindle often managed not to think about her trip. The Process, she had abandoned. Her collection of clippings about its inventor, her articles and notes were all underneath the liner paper in a kitchen drawer, but they might as well have been thrown away. At some point, she *would* throw them away but, at the moment, having to touch them might remind her of a man and what he did, and generally her life was freed from that.

Freed until dark. In the hardest place of the night when the same old fear of dying slipped over her in a fast, loose slither, when it breathed at her—then Edward was there, too. Curled on her side, with her face against the burn of the carpet, she shut up her eyes and was shown and shown again her age and max-imum possible time remaining, the losses and degen-erations that were seeping through already to cloud her life, and which would end in no more than a mem-ory of the lies she told and the darkness in her thoughts. Lies and thoughts of Edward would harden in her like old blood, and death would hollow her out into nothing but a soured and stiffened echo of herself.

Original Bliss

She would be all bad because of Edward—the battery-acid drip of Edward—the patient and poisonous shadow that showed her the way his forehead led his body when he turned, gave her the scent of his hand left in her skin and the impossible, racing feel of him that eased close with his breath on the telephone. And all of this was completely her own deliberate fault. She was harbouring the parts of him that stung, in under her eyelids and next to the prickle of appetite under her tongue. She couldn't balance her books for this, or for a holiday that was a lie and that was so much to do with the Flesh of a man and so little to do with the Spirit and the other Love she'd lost.

Alone after sunset, she was nothing but wrong ideas: wrong like they were again now, when a part of her wanted to say that if God didn't mean her to think in the way that she did, then He shouldn't have made her able to. God ought to be fair. If His divine intention had been to keep her inside His laws, He should never have left her to cope with things alone, or have teased her with a few days' respite before slapping her down again. She had been by herself and very tired for too long and not even saints could always manage that.

Mr. Brindle had a habit of telling her about saints.

"Suicide is suicide. They murder themselves and then everybody paints their portrait, names their bloody kids after them."

"They're examples."

"Crap."

"They are examples."

"Okay, fine, they're examples. So you have thousands of examples of how you're supposed to behave and how you're supposed to think and all of the rules you're supposed to follow. So why don't you go to church any more? Hm?"

"You know why."

"Aye, you're right I know why. I know fine why. You came to your senses. Creeping round here like Mrs. Fucking Jesus . . . I didn't marry that. Giving me that wee fucking Edinburgh smile every time I fucking swear."

"That's not—"

"What? True? You wanted me and you got me and now you've to fucking live with me when *I know you.* You're fooling nobody. 'I've lost my faith, I've lost my faith.' You never bloody had any. You're forgetting, I saw. I saw the way you were, home from your pisshole bloody church. I saw the colour in your face. I knew. You only ever went there for a come. Sweating with your eyes shut, kneeling—you were having a fucking come. I know. You only knelt because you couldn't stand. Then God couldn't get it up any more so you left him. Right? Right?"

He didn't always get so angry, there'd been something on his mind that time and then she'd been stupid and tried to explain herself to him, to talk about what was between them and growing thicker and filling the house until it was difficult to breathe when they were both inside. Everything she'd ever read about disagreements and about marriages had told her that she should explain and she had tried. Wrong night, that was all, she'd picked the wrong night.

"Right? Right?"

Mr. Brindle had been holding her by the wrist, really lifting her by the wrist until she was standing and walking, stumbling beside him from the living-room into the corridor, into the kitchen. She spent a lot of time in her kitchen; it was the part of her house which felt most like a home.

Remembering when Mr. Brindle had opened the drawer was hard. Perhaps she hadn't seen, or had only heard the scrape of the wood and the clatter of the contents inside, or she could have been too confused to notice anything except that Mr. Brindle was still shouting and that shouting always made her feel confused. Or as if she would cry. Sometimes it made her feel as if she would cry.

When he put her hand in the drawer, she thought he was looking for something and turned to his face. Mr. Brindle was smiling in the odd, tight way that people do when they are nervous or embarrassed by someone's pain.

Of course later, she would find this caught in her memory, because Mr. Brindle had been embarrassed by *her* pain, which didn't arrive at once, but was on the way.

She listened to the shutting of the drawer and watched the effect of his effort shudder across his face, followed by a moment of stillness, almost puzzlement. There was a hot numbness in the fingers of her hand. Mr. Brindle dropped her wrist and stepped away, observing.

Then Mrs. Brindle wanted to sit down, except that she didn't because she also wanted to be sick and she had a quite bad headache which made her need to rub her temples. She tried to lift her hands and discovered that one wouldn't lift. It was stuck. A burst of nausea and a white, high sound happened when she pulled on her arm and then she looked at her fingers, the four fingers of her right hand that were already a slightly unfamiliar shape and bleeding and a little hidden by four flaps of sheared-away skin. She could see the light of one of her bones.

While she fainted, Mrs. Brindle was still figuring the whole thing through, so that when she turned back to consciousness, she knew what Mr. Brindle had done. He had taken her hand and closed it in a drawer. She had made his damage worse when she wrenched her fingers free without understanding where they were.

Mr. Brindle was kneeling on the floor and holding her round the shoulders, trying not to look at her bleeding, but slipping his eyes down and sideways all the same. He told her that he was sorry and she nodded and fainted again.

Original Bliss

It would have been best to take her to the hospital, but instead Mr. Brindle called their doctor and then drove to the surgery. Her pain was an intimate thing between them which they didn't need to share. Mrs. Brindle listened while her husband talked about a horrible domestic accident and she then sat extremely still while her doctor explained that two of her fingernails would have to be removed. He would first give her ring injections—appropriate for fingers—which he hadn't practised since his student days, but he would do his very best.

Mr. Brindle waited outside while the needle went in and the scalpel cut and the blueing nails were tugged amazingly, easily away. She thought for a moment how softly she was put together. Then her wounds were dressed, splinted, turned into plump, clean fabric. Afterwards, the doctor looked for a long time at her face, but she couldn't tell him anything, even though both of them knew she wanted to.

Funnily enough, the kitchen hardly ever reminded her of that day. Mr. Brindle had cleaned her blood off the drawer himself and she would have had to study it carefully to see the denting in the wood. Now it was only the place she kept her tea towels safe: soft, clean, fabric things.

Edward had been able to hold her hand and find nothing strange about it, because it was fine now. More than two years of healing had made it useful and strong again. She didn't brood on what had once hurt it, because there was no point. But she did sometimes remember what she had thought of while she listened to her nails come away. Mrs. Brindle had considered how deeply she believed that marriage was a sacrament and that no one should act against a sacrament. Mr. Brindle did not treat marriage sacramentally. This meant that, in many important ways, she was not married to him.

This was a bad thing to think, or an odd thing to think, but not un-useful. In a way, it made her feel free enough to be able to stay and lie beside Mr. Brindle at the start of her nights, hearing the rustle of his hairs against her sheets. Inside she was free. She was staying and lying and knowing that she was free and not married to him.

Then Edward sent a postcard.

When he had almost become a person who was more in her mind than in recollections of reality, Edward got in touch. Five weeks after Stuttgart he wrote to her, on the whole of one side of a postcard that showed a view of night-time London and was sent inside an envelope.

Dear Helen,

For a while I thought it would be better not to write, but then I was sure you wouldn't write either. That made me sad. I am so sorry for being irresponsi-

ble. I thought you deserved the truth about me when you'd told me the truth about you. Now I think I thought wrong.

I hope you are well and happy Helen. Tell me if you are not. I repeat my address below in case you have lost it.

Do tell me if you are not.

Edward.

Helen put the card in her coat pocket and went out to walk. A fine summer was finally breaking and dusty rain fell out of an almost blue sky. It didn't bother her. Inside her pocket, she ran her thumb across the gloss of the photograph and then the polite friction of the writing surface; a postcard in an envelope, because all of the writing was for her and she had a husband and Edward had perfectly understood, without being told, that Mr. Brindle did not know about him and that Edward should not help him to find out.

She tried to think of what to do and couldn't. An uneasy tiredness dropped close in around her and she took another turn away from the house and then another again and there was no way she could write back to Edward and no way she could not.

Helen walked and discovered new details in herself. As far as she understood her God and His opinions, He would think it was bad for her to be tempted but worse for her to be disappointed that she hadn't given in. Nevertheless, she was sad that she had no hope of escaping the straight and narrow way and now that she'd resisted temptation, what little of God had returned to her was receding. God no longer needed to keep her from urgent sin and, because He didn't want her for Himself, He'd left her alone. He had abandoned her again and never explained Himself, never said why, that's what hurt her most.

She was beginning to think that relationships were possibly not her strong point. She couldn't manage one with God, or with her husband; she didn't like her sister and her parents were both dead. That only left Edward and all of her books—including the Good one—would advise her against him. He was not well. He'd admitted that. He had tastes with which she could not agree and which didn't even seem to please him, only to have power in his life. His not wanting to like what he liked made him a less than hopeless case but, nevertheless, Helen knew that damaged people often sought each other out and fell in love with their mutual diseases, to the detriment or destruction of their hopes and personalities. There were whole books about each part of that progression and the misfortunes of those trapped in repeating behaviours and bad relationships. Helen was attracted to a sick man; she was therefore sick. Edward was attracted to Helen; he was therefore sick. Helen was even sicker for knowing he was sick and still wanting him and yet, oddly, she felt very well for somebody so sick.

How was Edward attracted, that was what she didn't

know. It was none of her business, but she did want to know. He hadn't said why he was writing, or hadn't said clearly.

Without noticing, she had made her way back to her gate. Mr. and Mrs. Brindle's garden gate that defended Mr. and Mrs. Brindle's garden, around Mr. and Mrs. Brindle's domestic home. Soon she would stand in their garden, sheltered in the lee of the house and tear up the card with its envelope and burn them both, the powdery rain still falling about her silently.

She buried the ash.

Dear Mrs. Brindle,

   Dear Helen,

   I won't do this again. Having received no reply from you and having waited this reasonable while, I became unable to provide a sufficiently definitive explanation for your silence. I write now because another silence on your part will allow me to know that any explanation is no longer relevant. Or rather, that I am no longer relevant to you and should develop a little silence of my own. The rest of this letter will be about that so perhaps you need not read beyond this point.

   Of course, I hope you do. I personally am curious. I can't help reading anything once I've started. But then you know that. I can't help most things once I've started. I can work the Process for anyone but myself.

   So I have resorted to the standard, really rather

brutal methods that might be suggested for my recon-
ditioning. The brutality appeals to me: seems suitable
and good for the satisfaction of my self-disgust. In case
you were interested, I look at my pictures having
injected myself subcutaneously with 6mg of Apomor-
phine. The injection causes nausea unrelieved by vom-
iting, at least in theory. This means I should associate
my sexual obsession with nausea, rather than orgasm.
No carrot, all stick. I watch my videos while sniffing
valeric acid—vile stuff—and once again hope for suc-
cessful results. These rigmaroles seem to be taking
effect, they undoubtedly make me feel more lonely
than I have in several years. All the old friends going.

I do intend to become more normal.

That sounds alarming, doesn't it? Like some terri-
ble pervert whining. Really, I simply want my free
time back again, my time for hobbies and work and
the people that I like.

I want to be able to stand full in your eyes without
what I might describe as shame. I wish I could put
that more convincingly, but I can't.

All of which has little to do with your difficulties
and a great deal to do with my self-obsession. I have
been reading on your behalf, you know. Here is a
quote for you: "Ne demande donc pas la foi pour pou-
voir prier ensuite. Prie d'abord, et la foi inondera ton
âme." Someone called Grillot de Givry, with whom
you might identify. He suggests, if I can presume a
translation, that you don't ask for faith to pray later,

but pray first and faith will flood your soul. This sounds quite encouraging and is several hundred years old. I'm sure you've read him already; I'm sure I'm being no help here. As usual.

Actually, what I am doing is talking too much because I am nervous. I thought I should tell you something, that's all. On the fourth of next month I will be in Glasgow. There's a little two-day thing going on up there which I might attend. Equally, I can stay away, if I'm told to.

If you don't write and give me a yes or a no, then I won't know what to do.

Unfair of me to say so, but true.

Edward.

"I didn't think you would."

Edward appeared happy, but his mouth was tense. She thought it seemed tense. The over-illuminated air of the hospital canteen eddied round them as colour-coded human beings went to and from their curing and quieting tasks. Helen noticed she could taste, increasingly clearly, other people's panic and exhaustion and her own confusion, welling in. When Gluck stood up to meet her, he'd shaken her hand, very formal and far away. But when he caught at her eyes, he didn't seem formal, hardly even polite.

"Um, didn't think I would what?"

She couldn't read him, not clearly, not yet.

"Write. Of course. That's why I'm here."

"You wouldn't have come anyway."

"No." They caught themselves perusing each other and stopped at once.

"Really?"

"Yes, really." His voice sounded thin and vaguely

petulant. "Sorry, I didn't mean to be abrupt. I'm not making a good impression and I do want—" He clawed between his collar and his neck with one hand. "Sorry. Look, let's walk. I've had more than enough of this place. I should never have suggested we meet here. I might as well have dragged you out to the local abattoir; dignity and privacy, meat-hooked. Oh, I don't even want to think about it. Let me . . ."

He elbowed forward across the table, trying to slide inside his own anecdote. "You know they had therapeutic rabbits here?"

His face seemed very slightly thinner and very slightly afraid. She nudged at his knuckles, just to say *hello*. He chanced a smile. "Rabbits."

"Rabbits?"

"Mm. Lots of them. Participating patients could have one of their very own to care for, be fond of, give a name to—as you do."

They were both smiling now, they'd remembered they could do that.

"Nice."

"Yes. Then the last time they had a conference here, the caterers screwed up. No food for the Sunday evening."

"Don't tell me."

"Oh, yes." He sneaked in a whisper at her ear, the heat of it bleaching the meaning away from his words. "The psychiatrists ate the therapeutic rabbits, every one."

Then he dodged back, apparently uneasy again.

"Let's go." She tried to sound calming while remembering the bludgeon and tease of his breath. "I mean, would you like to go?"

"Yes, thank you. And if the shrinks want to burn me in effigy while I'm away, I am quite agreeable. They're exactly the types to believe in that kind of thing. Voodoo specialists. Sorry. I'm not going to get annoyed again. I'm going to leave."

Edward stood up and dragged his chair aside loudly, frowning down at the furniture that hemmed him in. Helen moved over to join him and rubbed at the small of his back.

"Oh." He sounded on the verge of pain. "That's . . . thank you. But—"

She stopped before he could tell her to.

"No, don't stop." Edward lightly took her hand and replaced it, stood while Helen rubbed again and tried to think how she had done this un-selfconsciously.

"Edward?"

"Yes." He faced forward: scanning, challenging the room.

"Are you all right?"

"I'm . . ." He reached his arm to lock it round her back. She stopped moving, just held. "I'm all right, yes. I am simply too angry, having spent a whole morning surrounded by drug-company reps." He kept staring out, but slightly increased the pressure of his arm about her. "You know what I put down as my hobbies in *Who's Who*?"

"No."

"Laughing at Classical Ballet and drug-company reps."

"I see." That sounded a stupid response, but she'd never met anyone else who'd been put in *Who's Who* and she'd never held Edward before, not for this long. Stupidity was all she could muster.

"This room is full of them: reps. So we shouldn't really stand like this . . ."

"Why not?"

"It will make them excited."

"They get easily excited?"

"They lead extremely sheltered lives. I mean, look at them—not exactly the faces of men who get lucky." He lifted his arm with a final, jingling brush at her spine. "Not that I'd know. How are you?"

"Okay." She thought she wouldn't move away from him just yet, because she wouldn't be able to touch him this way again.

"No. I said 'How are you?' " He finally faced her.

"Tired."

"I stopped you sleeping again, didn't I? Because I am a stupid bastard and sometimes it shows. I shouldn't have—"

"I came home. I don't sleep at home."

"Okay. But you look well, though. Trust me, I'm a

doctor. You do." He dipped in and kissed her cheek, retreating before she could make any response.

They left the hospital together and walked the straight and Great Western Road, in towards the Botanical Gardens and the town. Artfully displayed interiors posed through drawing-room windows and Gluck was mainly silent, although sometimes impressed by the sternly grey perspectives of Calvinist pseudo-classical façades.

"This is all very nice. Not like London."

"No, not like London. This is bad old money, but with good old style, because it's Scotland. We have style."

"You're a Nationalist?"

"No, a realist. It's just true."

Helen stumbled through her mind for useful things to say and noticed they were practically trudging now—this was too long a walk to be welcoming or sociable. She was getting it wrong, so many different kinds of wrong.

Gluck inhaled hard. "I do apologise."

"What for?"

"The mood I'm in. Mental hospitals make me very uneasy . . . well, furious. Which is decidedly unwise—they're the one place where no one should seem to be in imminent need of sedation, and I always do. And it is . . . not good to be with. Very unattractive and I'd rather be . . ."

"Attractive."

"Well, now you mention it . . . Probably. Something like that."

"You are attractive."

"Now I didn't say it because I wanted you to—"

"I know. That's one of the reasons you are. Attractive. I'm sorry, I shouldn't say."

"No. Quite likely you shouldn't."

Edward began to walk a touch ahead. She hadn't thought until now that he must have been slowing his pace down to hers.

Every time a bus churned by, Helen wanted to apologise for its noisiness, for the intrusion, for the fact that it destroyed whatever atmosphere they might have been creating. Not that any atmosphere she could think of was actually taking shape. This was her home territory, she ought to be able to welcome him and be entertaining about a place he'd never visited before, but she couldn't. She hoped for a light inspiration that could kick off some safer, smaller talk, but nothing came. The skin above her eyes felt sensitive and tense.

"Ach God, this is awful. Oh, I'm sorry."

She discovered she was holding Edward's hand, soft around the curl of his fingers. They had reached a standstill and he was looking at her flatly, his mouth tight.

"Oh, I didn't mean to say—I hate trying to make conversation. I think if you have to make it then you shouldn't be bothering. But I want to make it. I mean I think that I do want to talk. I don't know what to do here, Edward, do you know what to do here?"

Edward freed himself from her and then slid his hands up to touch either side of her face. He held her along the jaw and beside her cheeks, fingers mildly chill as they slipped to the start of her neck. His pressure was firm but trembled slightly. Hard under her breastbone, a type of fluidity seemed to break out; it lurched and then sparked away into a heightened, untrustworthy peace. She watched him and he watched her, because they were fixed in a position where they could do nothing else, although this was almost unbearable. When Edward spoke, Helen focused her attention on his lips to steady her concentration and found this didn't work. He had good lips.

"Helen, we've forgotten we know each other. I think that's all. No, it's not. I'm afraid that I seem disgusting now—because of the way I've behaved today—"

"No, really—"

"Then because of Germany—what I told you—what I do—and I find that I care about you more when I can see you than I did when I was thinking about you and I don't want to be disgusting and, Jesus Christ, Helen, I'm only a genius, I can't be expected to cope with this. With being confused." He rubbed his forehead. "I don't like to be confused."

"I know how you feel."

She touched his hands for the sake of touching them and at once he let go of her face. That seemed a shame.

"Look, I was going to drag you off to the Gardens . . ."

His hands tugged down against hers as she lifted them, the palms and thumbs and fingers, all made alive and in keeping with the proportions of the man.

"The Gardens up ahead there . . . and I'd have made you look at the squirrels when they're really just rats with a perm and cheeky to boot. I think we shouldn't do that. I think I should go home."

"Really?" He was trying to be unhurt, just the way he'd tried not to notice when she said *home*. He didn't understand about her home and how she and Mr. Brindle would define that word in ways that disagreed.

She squeezed and tickled at his palms. "That was in the wrong order. Sorry. I'm going home because then I'll come back out again. Right at the corner on this side of the street there's a big hotel with a bar. You'll find it no bother and I'll see you in there at . . . I will try to come and see you there at eight o'clock. If I'm late it means I couldn't get away, so don't wait. I'm sorry to be so uncertain. I will try."

"I understand."

. . .

"How was your sister?" Mr. Brindle was watching the Saturday sport on Mr. Brindle's TV set, from Mr. Brindle's chair. "Still depressed?"

"Yes. She's not doing well."

Although hardly anything was different in the living-room, Mr. Brindle made it untidy, surly, and somewhere she could only intrude.

"She needs to take herself in hand. She can't go through life expecting to be helped all the time. Even if her sister does have her heart set on playing the fucking saint."

She could be sure he'd hardly moved since she left him after lunch: sitting, sunk into the scrappy jeans and the sweatshirt and the stocking feet. He was wearing white socks. One day at home for white socks without slippers and they're done.

While she moved across the kitchen, she began to call through what she needed to say.

"Would you mind—"

"What does she want now?"

"I don't have to." She filled the kettle, switched it on, came back to lean in the doorway and stare at the back of Mr. Brindle's head.

"You don't have to what?"

"Saturday night on her own—it makes her feel lonely."

He turned to her. "And it won't do the same to me?"

"I don't have to."

"Ach, go on. Why not. Why not." He waved her over with his hand until she stood beside him and he could loop his arm in tight round the tops of her thighs. "Will you be late? You don't need to be late."

"No, I won't be late. I don't have to go."

"I can watch the film. It's decent, for once. Give her my best. Ho, ho."

"Yeah, right." She stooped down to kiss him and was sure, as her lips read his cheek and she smelt sleep on his skin, that she was betraying him. To kiss and betray. She would never have thought herself so far beyond help, but there she was, bending to him with a biblical condemnation like cold leather at her back— kissing to betray a trust.

Mr. Brindle glanced up to her, smiling, and stretched to give his own, answering kiss.

Helen was dressed for visiting her sister who was not in Glasgow and could not be visited; this meant she was not dressed for Edward, or even for the hotel bar. She felt indelibly ugly as she waited for her vision to adjust from a rather beautifully violent sunset to an interior gloom. The last time she'd had to pause like this, obviously searching for someone and at risk of disappointment, she'd been no older than twenty. Perhaps she appeared to be faking an elaborate absence of partner that would be the beginning of a come-on to the room. She knew there were glances evaluating and probably discounting her already as she tried to turn smoothly and take in all the tables where Edward might be. She was slightly late; he might have gone.

At least no one she knew ever came here, it was safe. No one she knew—she couldn't argue with that. Mr. Brindle had made sure there really was no one she knew: only the paper-shop man and the butcher and all of the other people she paid out Mr. Brindle's money to. She couldn't remember when she'd given up the struggle of trying to stay friendly with the last of her friends. Whatever they'd been able to give her was never worth what Mr. Brindle made her pay. Some of the churches had called sometimes, but not recently.

"I'm sorry, did I give you a start? You looked right past me twice."

The bar turned back to its various preoccupations and she let Edward lead her aside towards the furthest wall. A ridiculously piercing light made a tight hoop on the table-top. If they leant forward, their faces were bleached blank, or troubled with odd shadows.

"I'm late."

"I know. I was just going."

"Were you?"

"No. I was just preparing to spend a very long night getting maudlin drunk on my own. Tell me about how you are, Helen, all about that. Did any of what I suggested help?"

She had expected he might be angry when she told

him that she'd abandoned the whole of his Process and gone back to her nights spent with death. But Edward was only sad. From time to time, she would mention a detail from her home or from the particular style of living she had made and a shiver of discomfort would close Edward's eyes or make him stare away. He found her life far more unpleasant than she could.

If he asked her questions, they were gentle, but precise in a way that meant she answered them without evasion or concealment. Perhaps for as much as an hour, he was with her in her thinking, as if they were dreaming together, or of each other.

When she had no more to say, he let her watch him while he made her a part of his work, an element in what was the brightest and closest part of him. His expression died away to something more than sleep, a lonely consideration that took the colour and the pupils of his eyes and deepened them together into one, dark thing that saw and saw and saw. His voice sank in his chest, solid and low. He ripped pages from his notebook, covered them in tiny, regular print and gave them to her. He asked her to repeat certain instructions and orders of action and she did so, as if she were taking oaths of allegiance to a country they intended to create. Last of all, he made her laugh.

"That's better. I don't mind being serious, but I draw the line at solemn. And I'm tense enough as it is.

Don't want to mess up again." He paused for an unnecessary breath. "There's nothing else I have to suggest, but at least now I can feel I've done my duty properly."

Helen dropped her head while her smile couldn't help squeezing down into something grey. "I didn't know I was a duty."

He reached immediately for her hand, but then didn't touch it. "You're not. See—I'm messing up already? *That* was my duty, but *you* are not and now I can talk *to* you, instead of *about* you. I mean, I could have written you a letter with all this." He prodded the pile of notes with his finger. "Couldn't I?"

"Mm hm."

"But that wouldn't have been as good."

"No."

"Look at me. Okay. Now shall we enjoy ourselves? Would that be the right thing to do?"

Helen sat at rest while a swipe of vertigo pressed through her. She no longer had any grip on the right thing to do. She had no idea of anything but what she wanted, and what she wanted was not an idea. Considering what might stop her from doing wrong, or what might make her hold on morality even more precarious, she said, "You could tell me about you."

"How do you mean?"

"We've talked about my problems . . ."

He eased out half a sigh. "I said in my letter, I've

been trying all the nasty old tricks I've just spent my morning preaching against: drugs that make me sick, foul smells, electric shocks—"

"Shocks?"

"Helen, if I thought it would help, I'd sit and watch mucky videos while beating a steel mallet off my head. Any unpleasant stimulus will do. The trouble is . . . do you really want to hear about this, because I may enjoy telling you in a way that I should not."

"I don't believe that."

"Because you believe in confession?"

"Because I think you're trying to be different. And maybe . . . I'm curious."

"Curious. Well, then I should tell you everything, of course." There was a brittle line in the way he said that. She'd forgotten how easily she could hurt him and how little she wanted to.

"Not that—"

"No, no. You're curious, that's fine." He stared at the table and began a sharp, low monologue. "So I should start with what? Number of times I come in one day? An average day? Six. Everything else has to fit around that number: where I go, how long I can stay, what work I can do, what excuses I make to slip away, what possible material I can get that will still have an edge, that will still manage to stimulate me when I've already seen every bloody thing there is. Have you ever sat up late at night when you should have been marking papers for a third-year exam and watched a German Shepherd licking Pedigree Chum off a cunt before fucking it? Good film, terrific reviews—if you read the same papers I do."

He wasn't being angry with her; she had to bear in mind that he wasn't being angry with her.

"Or the guy who loves to fist them, gets in there up to his wrist, has a preference for cunts and doesn't mind the blood. Or actually, I beg your pardon, he *likes* the blood and I *don't like* any of this at all, but I have to have it because anything else doesn't work any more. I watch men shoving Perrier bottles where the sun will never shine and part of me hopes that the bottles don't break, but only a small part, because the rest of me is watching. I always have to watch. No matter what.

"Even if it hurts. Do you know how many times I can wank before it starts to hurt? I know exactly, but that isn't where I stop. Some drug addicts in withdrawal, they have the same problem. I've written monographs on it: the fascinating phenomenon of forcing yourself to shoot your load over and over again, even though every time you touch yourself it makes you want to scream. Still, I wouldn't wish to exaggerate, that only happens every month, or so.

"And I am trying to fight it, I'm doing my best with the aversion therapy . . . Aversion—that's a joke. I'm going through all the steps, every spell and potion for de-conditioning success, but I already loathe what I do. I can't hate it any more completely and I still don't stop. Jesus, I'm even starting to like the electric shocks—I associate the charges with being about to ejaculate. Still curious?"

"Of course, if you're going to be angry, then you won't be anything else."

"What?"

"Mr. Brindle does it all the time: gets angry. It's something people do instead. I don't know what he really is, but he gets angry instead. I think you don't want to be ashamed."

Edward wrapped his arms tight around his ribs, exhaled and inhaled again. "Ten out of ten. Ten out of ten. You might want to add in that I would also rather not be afraid. Obviously I am."

"Why."

"Why?" His voice sounded tiny, surprised. "Because I don't want you to go."

"That's . . . something good."

"It might not always be."

"Mm hm."

"And I need you. You're one of my cures. The best of them, in fact. Pain and nausea I know about—I know all about—but if I can talk to you, I remember it later. When I open up a magazine, when I put in a video, I remember you and I can't . . . I get too ashamed. It's good. To be humiliated."

Edward rubbed at the back of his neck, then reached for her hand again, took it and pulled it smoothly along the table-top. Helen sat very slightly nearer while he rubbed his thumb across the root of her fingers, worked into the shallow fold of skin behind the knuckle and inside the tidy dark of her closed fist.

"You wouldn't believe how easily it started. I was fresh back from America, very young, very promising and I didn't have time for a person to be in my life. I was busy building myself into a genius and finding out how easy that could be and there was so little space for everything necessary, I quite frequently went without sleep. But then again I have never been devoid of feelings—sexual impulses—I've always had what most people have—the desire to be with someone. I've often wanted to love.

"I'd never thought that buying people, hiring them, would be a way forward for me; not because of scruples, I was just scared of diseases and of being caught. The books, the magazines, I could use them according to my schedule, they seemed perfectly convenient and unshameful. Naturally, at that point I didn't quite realise I'd end up having private carrier's lorries arriving to dump shifty, plain, brown packages, addressed for only me, at every house and research establishment I would ever be associated with.

"It has to be a private carrier, you see—Her Britannic Majesty's mail won't deliver my style of literature—the illegal kind. It comes under the same regulations that prevent you from posting shit. Obscene and Offensive Material.

"My life is neither wild, nor exotic, just massively embarrassing."

He grabbed at his glass and found it empty; this appeared to puzzle him.

"Did I drink that?"

"Yes, I think you did. Edward, you want to change, that must make a difference. You'll find out how to do it and it'll work. You're a genius—that's what you're for."

"Yeah." He frowned at the buttons of ice left in his tumbler, shook them.

"I wish I could help you."

"You *do* help. Really—you are already helping me. I came up here without any kind of dreadful material and I've been okay. I made it. That's . . . more than twenty-four hours since I looked at anything." He searched her expression to see if she understood. "I haven't done that in years. Obviously, it doesn't mean too much; I could remember enough to see me through, if I tried." She watched him frown to himself and wished he needn't. "But I haven't tried. I've been . . . quieter. I've been thinking about you, instead." He brushed her arm quickly. "I mean of what you would think, your disapproval. I should have asked you if I could, though, shouldn't I? If I could think of you?"

"It's your mind, you can think about what you like in it. And I did say I wanted to help."

He kissed at the top of her head. "You're good, you

are." His face seemed terribly lonely, with a light of hunger to it. "Anyway, this may sound quite unimpressive, but I walked all the way through two different railway stations today and I didn't buy a thing. And bear in mind that when I'm travelling I do make a habit of buying things in this particular area." He breathed out a dull laugh. "Moral turpitude governs my travel arrangements far more effectively than any tourist agency. In Europe and America, I take an extra bag—for reports and research, that's supposed to be—but I bring it back home full of filth, my favourite. Customs hassle me sometimes, that's all.

"In Britain, I have a weakness for railway stations. Well, they're so romantic." He didn't smile. "And they're where I started out, because they're ideal. They have everything waiting for me: *The Story of O*, true-life sex crimes, pathology with pictures, *Justine*, top-shelf magazines you can buy in armfuls because no one knows you and no one cares and any possible disapproval will not stick. These places are nowhere, they don't count, so I can be anyone I want to—be disgusting—be quite openly what I am."

"You are not disgusting."

"It's kind and completely unrealistic of you to say so."

"Edward, please."

He laid his hand above hers and she felt him warm and then the cool of him lifting softly away. She heard him clear his throat to speak, to murmur in close at

her cheek. "In Glasgow today I went from the plat-
form and into a taxi, without even looking for the
bookstall, not a glance. My hotel doesn't have a soft-
core channel. I did check. I don't think you *have* any
sex shops that I could search for. So I'm fairly safe.
No." He paused and let her cheek touch the shape of
his mouth. "I'm very safe—you're here. So I'll be
good."

She eased her arm in round his shoulders because
she needed to and it also seemed the proper thing to
do. Edward leaned back against her. She felt it when
he exhaled, understood the sudden flex and rub of his
neck. The surprising weight of his head rocked against
her.

"Tired?"

"Exhausted, actually."

Helen enjoyed how comfortable and comforted she
was with this man in an almost-embrace, with the shift
and the change of his bones, his breath. An emotion
resembling fear prickled at the small of her back,
threatened, then withdrew again.

"It's odd." Helen wasn't speaking to make sense,
only to be speaking, to keep some limitation between
them, a boundary of words. "It's odd."

"You can say that again." Edward tried a chuckle
and then they both rocked inside it together long after
the sound had gone. "You did, though, didn't you?
Always thinking ahead." The back of his neck rubbed
against her again, at home with her in a sleepy, dis-

turbing way. "Oh, Helen. You're a good person. What are you doing here with me?"

She turned to meet his stare but couldn't hold it. "I'm being where I want to. And I'm not all that good. I just don't often do what I want."

"Is what you want bad?"

"Sometimes."

"What kind of bad?"

Something bloomed at the back of her thinking like an unpredictable pilot light. "I don't know."

Although it was very gentle, very milky, she could feel Edward's voice shake low and solid against his ribs. "You must know, it's what you want."

Helen tugged her arm from behind him and sat forward to the table-top. "When I was at school, I used to read up on the sexual diseases. They were so correctly frightening; things like syphilitic aneurysms, I never forgot about them. If you had bad sex, wrong sex, then your blood vessels would balloon up in your chest and finally burst. You would explode inside because of badness; because of men and badness and that seemed absolutely fair."

"You only get syphilis from someone else with syphilis." He was making an effort to sound authoritative. "I mean that's a . . . fact." But he ended in a stagger of consonants. "An absolute . . . Hmn."

"I know, I'm just saying that when I was young I was always afraid that even if I thought too much about it, about men, I'd balloon. Everyone told me how terrible sex was and how men might do anything and I would wonder about that anything—what it would be like—and then I would worry that I'd burst."

"But you didn't. You can't have thought bad enough things."

"I suppose not. There's time yet, though."

"True. And I'm a bad influence."

"Yes."

Their silence surprised them, left them undefended, suddenly. Edward rubbed lightly at his arm and watched her face.

They thought for a moment and then they agreed themselves into a kiss, the open-mouthed soft and hard kiss with him she now realised she'd very often thought about. For some considerable time, they were both lifted up in far too much breathing and in her touching the gallop of pulse at his throat and the soft heat at his collar and the whole, continuous shape of him while they touched—Edward not incautious, not discourteous. They did not hurry, only ached towards each other, in the grip of babbling neurones and unruly electricity.

"Well, then." Edward smoothed against one of her breasts very slightly as he moved to close his arms on her again; the accidental but un-accidental nice experiment. "I had hoped—" He sighed slowly so it would catch in her hair. "You must tell me what we're going to do. Helen? Are you still here?"

"Yes. Yes, I'm—You're very . . ."

"So are you. Tell me. What do we do?"

Her hands met behind his spine and she held him as if he might print himself under her skin if she gave him enough of her pressure and her time. She couldn't, didn't want to speak.

"Helen. Please tell me. Either way." Silence licked between them. "It's no, isn't it?" The way he said it, she understood he'd been prepared for disappointment and understood that he deserved much better, but that she couldn't give it to him.

She had to look at Edward very clearly, so that he would know she was telling the truth. "Everything would have to be different and it's not. That's the only reason . . ."

"Does everything matter?"

"Don't make me argue. Please. I can't."

But Edward didn't make her argue, he shook Helen's hand over-gently and was too polite and telephoned for a taxi to take her home even though he was a visitor to her city and must have found that slightly difficult. When he came back to their table, she saw, really saw, how well he'd dressed and made an effort for her and she wanted to make efforts back and not leave him unhappy, not leave him.

"I'm sorry, Helen. Again. Intellectually, with people I can be . . . I can out-perform anyone. But I know I'm not good at touching."

"That isn't—"

"That's fine. I know. Don't worry."

He worked himself into his coat, struggling slightly with one of the sleeves. When she reached to help him, he stepped aside. "No. It's okay."

Of course, she was too late home.

Helen scrubbed and laundered out the reek of Edward E. Gluck, the untouchable tang of herself with him. Only her jacket remembered him clearly, she couldn't make the time to dry-clean it, or had no wish to find the opportunity. Still, even there his scent faded; the pitch and throb at her stomach when she moved the cloth died quite away. The impossible had no shelf-life, couldn't last.

Cooking was the thing now—a blessing, perhaps literally. Mr. Brindle was a highly particular eater, always had been. It was necessary to please him, but beyond that basic requirement, Helen could find a certain self-expression and an occupation for her time. Her choice of menus came to rely on increasing allowances for preparation. Overnight marinating, standing, resting, proving, reduction and clarification—they all encompassed a type of waiting, a business that need not interfere with thought, or the active avoidance of thought.

Original Bliss

A clever choice of dishes might see her washing up the breakfast ruins, Mr. Brindle having duly gone to work, and then inching out the whole day with tiny exercises in perfectionism. Happily, her efforts were rewarded with fairly consistent success and she could feel that she was doing her best, making a go of it, of Mr. and Mrs. Brindle, of them.

Her peace at the dinner table was bought in little accidents. Helen gave herself more time to work, but also became more careless. Her concentration was poor and she was continually burning herself with pot lids, sugar syrup, steam. Opened cans and the good knives she had bought a long time ago—as an investment and as things to make her glad—slashed at her palms and fingers. She used the bright blue colour of dressing recommended for kitchens, because they cannot be lost in foodstuffs by mistake. Mr. Brindle made her change them when he was in the house. He did not want a wife whose hands were ridiculous.

But he did want a wife. Mr. Brindle had taken to touching her more than she could remember he ever had. At times when she could not expect it, his arm would thump in around her waist, or he would pad up behind her and palm at her breasts. He never approached her at night now, never in their bed, but his sudden presences started to soak their home. He was like a flood. Helen would wake on the living-room floor and have to stand immediately to have her head safe above the flux and drift of something. Mr. Brindle spoke no more than usual, but left a new kind of silence, washing in behind him whenever he left her alone. The arrangements of her furniture slid towards the cramped and the uneasy, the submarine.

Dear Helen,

No more aversion—total abstinence. Much more to do with the Process: "more gentle and more terrible," as I do tend always to say.

This is my first day. I shall tell you of any others. I won't lie.

One day. Twenty-four hours.

Love, Edward.

And thank you for your help.

Love. A small word like scalpel or a pocket knife. She'd never been able to write it down and she couldn't tell from the writing whether Edward did it easily.

Another enveloped postcard. She didn't burn it. Too much water about in the air, it would never have caught.

Sinners were supposed to burn, but here she was drowning instead, sinking in something that pounded up fast at blood-heat into what was already her standing pool of a house. She had never realised she was like this, had never been this kind of woman in her life. The World and the Flesh and the Devil, they were all supposed to tempt, but the Flesh had never troubled her before. Helen was not used to thinking of her own flesh and the way it would ask inappropriately for the flesh of someone else. Helen hadn't known about undersea nights, layered with the salt ghosts of lip and tongue and touch.

> *Dear Helen,*
> *Seven days.*
> *Thank you.*
> *Love.*

Mr. Brindle fed avidly, but never grew fat. Only dense and quiet, like a low-tide rock.

> *Dear Helen,*
> *Almost slipped away there, but didn't.*
> *Eighteen days.*
> *Love,*
> *Edward.*

If God was God, then He could see right in through her, as if she might just as well be a window or a Russian doll made out of glass. If God was God, He stood outside of time, so that everything she'd ever done was stacked up inside her for Him to count like chips she'd used to back the wrong number, the wrong bet. God knew her complete, the finished facts of all she'd do until she died, and she was either forgiven now or she was not and that was the way it would be and had been, forever and ever, amen. Whatever she did, God had watched her already, doing it.

Now and again, as she thought of Edward, Helen's good fear, her God fear, would tease and dazzle back towards her. Wrapping chicken thighs in smoked bacon, she had paused and understood that yesterday when she stood in the same place and stared through her ghost reflection in the same window, she had been deep in her usual, stable, lack of faith. Today she was convincingly afraid. She heard the falling sheet-metal din of Heaven's terror on all sides, shivering and slicing with the wonderful clarity of God and then, like any storm, it passed.

Thirty days.
  Dear Helen,
  A whole month.
  I am happy. Hope you are the same.
  Love,
    Edward.

Mr. Brindle did not like his Greek honey pie. There was too much salt in the pastry which had been correct for the recipe but not for his tastes. He didn't shout at her, only asked for a piece of fruit and a glass of water to clean his mouth. She went and fetched them as quickly as she could, thick currents tugging and struggling at her legs.

Original Bliss

Helen,

I celebrated my month the wrong way.

Back at six days now. Think I have learned from this.

I let you down, didn't I?

Sorry, Edward. And love.

You deserved better. I know that. I will try.

Coincidences and earthquakes, they were acts of God. People didn't make them happen, they happened to people. If Edward was meant to happen then Edward was an act of God. Perhaps God disapproved of her staying here and only *thinking* of Edward when *being with* Edward was God's will.

This was difficult to think about. Helen polished the windows with newspapers and vinegar because they left no streaks and combed out the fringes on the Chinese rug they'd bought when Chinese rugs were still expensive. It was hard to imagine that Edward was God's intention. She would have been pleased to do God's will, obviously, but then thinking how much she might want to would make her restless. Helen found she could be impatient to serve God.

"I've been meaning to ask you . . ."

Helen was rinsing the last of the soap-suds from the kitchen sink. Out in the dark of the garden she could see the box of yellow brightness that pressed down across the grass from the lighted window. She watched as Mr. Brindle's shadow joined hers and then swallowed it.

"Ask me?"

"Mm." His chin settled in heavily at her shoulder while his hands stooped and caught at the hem of her skirt. "You don't mind, do you?"

"What?"

"This." He dragged up her skirt in one hard motion, turning it out like a sleeve, so it gathered up high round her waist. Then his weight forced back against her again, covering her with the cloth that covered him and taking the balance from her legs. Something tumbled in the cupboard under the sink.

"You don't mind. Open your blouse. No, I'll do it, you're tired. I can do it right."

She felt the first, hot tug. Buttons chattered everywhere on to different hard surfaces. She tried to remember where she heard them fall, so she could find them later and they wouldn't go to waste and Mr. Brindle ripped at the cloth of her blouse, dug his cold, blunt fingers under her bra and wrenched it up, squeezed at her, squeezed again, enjoyed a twist.

"Is he out there? Does he watch the house? Where does he live?"

"I don't know—"

"Shut up. Can he see me now, in my house, touching my wife, having my wife? Can he see? Answer me. Can he see?"

There was no point in saying. "Who?" There was no point in saying it, she knew.

"Who? *Who?* Who do you fucking think."

She felt the fumble and a shearing, unlikely pain.

"Edward. *Eighteen days and love* Edward. *Touching my wife in the street* Edward. *Get her back for another fuck later* Edward."

A final, hauling cut and release, the scratch of a raw nail from his finger.

"Feeling better? That's the way you like it, isn't it? With the knickers off? Did you smell them after the last time? I did. You cunt."

There'd been another night, years ago, when he'd hit her more. Then, Helen knew she'd done nothing, hadn't understood at all and so she'd been able, in a way, to defend herself. This time, she couldn't resist him, couldn't find the strength, because she was at fault and whatever happened, it was meant. God's will.

Lying on the linoleum in the wet of something, she kept still. To keep still was important. Invisible. She thought about invisible.

"Cunt."

She felt him open her and spit.

"Cunt."

She felt the beginning of the kick.

He usually stopped because he was tired, not because he wanted to.

"What's the matter? Helen?"

"Nothing." She hadn't thought she'd ever use his number. "I'm fine." Even when he gave it to her, the hurt behind his eyes had told her very clearly that he didn't believe she would call. "I just wanted to call."

"Well, that's . . . thank you. I'm very glad."

Her breath was coming in hot gouts. There was a plan she'd made for what to say, but it was slipping.

"That's all right. I wondered . . . I wondered . . ." The sentence failed her.

"Where are you? And are you okay, you don't sound it. Where are you, Helen?"

"Here."

And then she cried. It surprised Helen how very seldom she cried, but when the feeling was on her she did it a lot.

Edward wanted to come and get her, but she made

herself able to say she would go to the underground station at Gloucester Road and he could meet her. He said that wasn't too far from his house.

Although she had no doubts that he would be there, she worried he'd be late, or that she wouldn't see him, or would take the wrong way out. If he wasn't right on hand and ready to be recognised Helen knew she would start crying again and people who cried publicly in London were always mad; changing guards and ravens and the homelessly mad—that was the capital. Helen didn't want to be homeless or mad.

At the barrier she concentrated on lifting her bag ahead of her and feeding her ticket through correctly and on looking up only at the very last point she could.

Edward.

Edward making this home.

Edward making this safe.

She was taken by a liquid feeling that pained her while it pleased.

Edward, already sidling through the crowd, cautiously tall, rummaged at the top of his hair with one hand, indisputably there. He lifted her bag away from her, took her arm and was ready when she swung in and held him and was able to hold her back.

"Hello."

"Hello."

He was so much more of himself than she had remembered, even though she had tried to remember him well.

"Welcome to Bailey Park."

Helen felt him rest his mouth against her hair and knew that people were walking round them, thoroughly inconvenienced. She didn't feel guilty a bit.

Outside there was a dry, grey, bite in the air and unfamiliar leaves, big like crumpled sheets of brown paper, were softening the pavement. They walked to Edward's home, side against side, cradling each other's waists because for two people walking together, this is the most comfortable way to proceed.

"I won't consider it."

"I have money. I mean, I'll be able to get some. Tell me a good place to stay, that's all I need."

"Helen, you don't have any money, be sensible. You can be here."

"That's not why I called you."

"I know that. There's a room you can sleep in, *will* sleep in, and I will trust you, if you will trust me to do nothing but sleep. I'm hardly going to creep up on you in the dark—not one of my vices. If that's what was worrying you. I can't think of anything else, unless you just . . ." He burrowed his hands in each other uneasily. "You've come here because I'm your friend. I hope. I help my friends. *Aaaw, come on, Helen. Let me help you out and do like Jimmy would—I've never hayd the chaynce before.*"

"No, leave Jimmy out of it, I'm talking to you."

"Then let me be here for you, because I want to. Be here for me."

They weren't really arguing. The words were like an argument, but they didn't mean one.

"I can't."

"Do it anyway. There are so many other things you can't. You want a whole life full of *can't*s? Maybe this is one you can. Come on, it's harmless. Me too." Edward seemed to consider smiling, but then didn't want to risk it. He left the room instead, fumbling as he closed the door, and she knew he had gone to make up the bed where she would sleep.

She sat in Edward's living-room and listened to him scuffling softly in and out of other doors, opening drawers and bustling, moving inside a flat that was totally his. Everything here was built up and covered with years and years of Edward, uninterrupted by anyone else. He smelt of his flat, she realised, and his flat smelt of him and she was breathing easily, liking the taste of him in her lungs. She was coming up for Edward's air and finding it familiar and still. This was a good, soft place. Her hands, clasping tight to each other, were lit by the slightly disturbing high and wide window that still held the sky she'd seen behind him in one of his photographs.

At rest and with an emptying mind, she remembered how much she ached: because of the bruising and confusion and most of all with holding on, with clinging as hard as she could from the inside, so nothing of her personality could fall out of place. The concentration she had needed to force a way through the journey south had left her almost hypnotised with exhaustion. Sentences and images looped and repeated inside her skull, cut loose from any sense.

Slowly, she stopped trying to look all right. Mr. Brindle had been careful as ever to leave her face unmarked, but if she really wept, the hurt would show and now she wanted it to. Mr. Brindle had made the pain, but it was hers and she could do what she wanted with it at any time.

"Oh, don't. You don't need to. It's fine now. Unless you want. It's okay if you want." She hadn't heard Edward come in and couldn't think clearly how long he'd been gone.

Helen bleared up at him while he stumbled forward and patted at her. One of his hands was holding something. "I made toast."

For some reason this let waves of sobbing break up through her. She listened to herself. She wouldn't stop.

"Well, it's all . . ." He clattered the plate down on the table and tried to lever his arms in about her. "Toast is all I make. Helen. Helen?" She knew he was beginning to lift her, but couldn't help. For a moment he rocked her forward. "It's all right. You know it's all right."

They scrambled against each other, Edward making for the sofa until they hit it and fell. For a long time,

Helen was aware of being against him, his pullover and solid ribs. She touched him from inside a fog of her own noise.

Edward held her until she was quiet, until the sky in the window had bruised into an overcast night.

"Helen. Helen? You're not asleep?"

"No." She swallowed. Her throat was raw. "No, I'm here."

"Good. And I'm here, too. No." She turned and met the quiet tension in his arms. "Don't move. Just lie. I want to talk to you—it's nothing bad."

He began to kiss across her forehead, sometimes brushing away her hair because that was a good thing to do. "I wanted to say," he punctuated himself, "that you," with regular, "are exceptionally beautiful," tiny pressures of mouth, "and that you have," and breath, "a beautiful brain. I was incapable of saying this properly before. Because I can be almost terminally inarticulate when it comes to people. You know how I am—I do get it right, but only eventually. I count myself lucky that you're so patient.

"And now I have a duty to say that, inside here, in your mind, there's no limit to you. You are your own universe. Your own happiness. They could dye you with silver nitrate; you'd be your own photographic plate. A picture of the roots into your soul." Edward paused, nuzzling her hair.

"Networks. And webs. And branches. Layered. Woven. Spun out of need and hope and, um, love.

Love." The word caught at something in her blood. "You're free, Helen. You've always been free. If God made your mind, then that is the way that He made you. Now you're to stay here as long as you like. Nothing bad will happen, do you understand?"

"Okay."

She knew that when she spoke, her words touched his throat, the open button at the collar of his shirt and his neck.

"Whatever has, will . . . whatever happens, our mutual conditions are not at fault. That is to say, I can't second-guess God, but if I'd made you, I would wish you to be completely yourself and not necessarily perfect."

Her eyes stung out of focus and she shook her head against him. "It's all gone wrong."

"Oh, don't say that. Please. Not when you're here with me. This is the point where it starts to go right. Don't try to stop it. We can be safe here and . . . we'll have fun or something. Talk. You can have this. You don't have to pay for it—no more than you already have. You're not a bad person, Helen, not sinful. I don't think we even understand sin—what we commit and don't—we can't judge. We just should collate our total information, be complete and act for the best. We're for the best. We, meaning me and you. What do you say?"

She said *yes*, because she felt *yes*.

"Thank you, Helen."

"Why thank me?"

"Because you came to me." She tried again to sit up and this time he let her. "I mean thank you for knowing you'd be welcome. He grinned up at his ceiling and then down at her. "All the way to London with no guarantees . . . That Mrs. Brindle, she's a determined woman and she does get what she wants."

Helen thought of what she wanted and Edward's eyes stammered shut while his hands wrestled quietly with each other. "*Aaaw, yagodda see, I wish a was a little bit bedder at making folks feel okay. No practice.* James Stewart would do this better."

"But he wouldn't be the same as you."

Edward flushed mildly and began a contented frown. "Better luck next time."

"No thanks."

The cold toast was still on the coffee table, untouched. Edward stirred, "Well, I'm going to . . . If you would like to see your room. I don't know . . . are you tired?"

"Absolutely."

"Good. That is, you'll sleep, which is good. Will you?"

Helen nodded. Stood up and apart from him.

The room he offered her was lined with shelves and heavily curtained and carpeted. The small sounds she made unpacking her night things; coming back from his orderly bathroom that smelt so remarkably of his skin; undressing for bed—every tiny impact and footfall was damped down, softened to silence. He had given her somewhere insulated where she couldn't help but be at peace.

Their first breakfast developed the easy shape it would always have while she was there.

"Toast." Edward pointed at the toast plate in case she found it unfamiliar and seemed to wonder if he read his newspaper next or talked.

"It's all you can make."

He let go the paper and smiled. "Well remembered."

"You only told me last night."

"Nice to be remembered, though. Toast is, in fact, not absolutely everything I can make. It's nearly absolutely everything."

"Good. I can cook. But I don't like to."

"Fine. That's fine." There was a tremor in his hand. He noticed and rested it under his chin. "Sleep?"

"No thanks, I've just had one."

"Fine. Good." He leaned his chair back recklessly. "Well, I'm going to do some work now, since I have time to do that again. If you—" Feeling himself unsteadied, he swung into the table again. "You should treat this as where you live, as home. Do what you want. Bearing in mind that I'll take you out to eat. If you want to be taken . . . I won't *make* you eat . . . that is, obviously you *will* eat . . . but not necessarily with me. It's not a problem, um, evidently. In fact the only one confused here is me." He sighed lightly and began again. "If you do want to go with me, to eat, then we can co-ordinate times and things; it would be more efficient that way." He felt forward for the butter knife, something to distract him.

"Why did you put me in that room?"

Setting the knife back and numbly making sure that it was straight, "I know, I know. It *is* the spare room, it simply isn't all that spare. It's always been where I keep the stuff—everything's in there. I do apologise."

"It's like . . . a library . . ."

"I know. It's not good. You could stay in my study instead." He examined the palm of his hand with sudden concern. "I should have mentioned . . . And now I have to say that I am making use of you—of your presence—because it keeps me out of there. Not that I go in there any more, in amongst the muck. I'm behaving." He checked her eyes. "I am. But if you're there, even if you've *been* there, it will make me feel safe. I slept safe last night." He borrowed a glance at her, then blinked away. "But I should have asked your permission, I know."

"I slept safe, too."

"Oh. Well, good."

"How much is there?"

"How much . . .?"

"How much muck."

"Oh, as much as you could see. Four walls, from

ceiling to floor: videos, magazines, books." Edward seemed anxious to be comprehensive, keen to be humiliated with absolute accuracy. "There are some originals of *The Oyster* and *The Pearl* from when I was kidding myself this was all about art—bloody expensive stuff and no good, because Victorian tastes are not quite mine. Porn gets dated, like anything else. Which all helps me to side-step saying that I don't exactly know how much. I counted the videos once; there are seven hundred of them, seven twenty, something like that, but that's as far as I got. The act of cataloguing tends to become secondary. I start off alphabetical and then I go astray. I get too absorbed in my work." He was trying to keep it light, but his eyes weren't managing. "No self-control."

"You have control now."

"I try. Seeing it all offends you, doesn't it? I mean, the titles are bad enough. I'm sorry."

"I was surprised, that's all. It helps you if I'm in there?"

"Honestly?"

"Of course."

"I don't want to put you under pressure, but yes, it does."

"Well I might as well stay there, then. You're the one who'd have the problem being in there. I don't mind."

Edward twisted out a smile and rubbed his cheek.

"But why haven't you thrown it all away?"

He spoke with the air of a man describing an incorrigible friend. "Will-power." He rubbed his cheek again. "I decided I would test my will-power by keeping my temptations within reach. Otherwise they're hardly a temptation, after all . . ." His eyes searched the air above her. "Obviously, if my will then fails me, I can get really disgraceful pretty much instantaneously." Edward examined her expression almost surgically. "I know, I'm fooling no one, not even me. I know exactly what I'm like. I only ever assume the moral high ground to get a running start for my descent."

He huffed out a breath with something approaching relief, still bewildered by himself, but more content. "Positive action must be taken, I realise, I just can't take it yet. I do live in hope, though—I'm back to nearly a month without a slip and some days I don't even think of wanting it. Eventually, I'll be able to chuck it away. And I'll do the chucking, no one else." His mouth tensed. "By then I might have worked out how on earth to dispose of it. I can hardly stack it all down at the bottom of the stairs and wait for the bin men to come. If that isn't a slightly over-appropriate verb."

Edward began a stretch then faltered, stopped. She wanted to touch him a little and thought about how.

"Oh, God."

"Edward? What?"

"Oh, God. Helen. I didn't—"

Helen had pushed up her sleeves, as she often did. She had forgotten the scratches on her forearms, the random bruises, the finger-grip imprints. The marks were dark, ripe, full of blood.

"What did he do?"

"It's all right."

"No, it's not fucking all right. What did he do?"

She really didn't need him to be angry on her behalf, Helen was perfectly able to manage that herself, if she chose to; she was a determined woman, after all.

"What did he do?"

Edward was starting to frighten her and she couldn't allow him to. He was starting to shout.

"He found one of your postcards." She didn't say that to blame Edward, only to make him be quiet and just let her forget it again. "That's what he did. He found your card."

"Oh, Hele—"

"You'd have watched it, wouldn't you? If I'd been a video, you'd have watched."

Edward almost reached for her, but then let his arm withdraw. He closed both hands over his head and said nothing.

A person who is scared and angry often strikes out inappropriately. Helen wished that she didn't conform so perfectly to type.

. . .

They were civil to each other after that, but they didn't exactly speak. Edward shut himself into his study for most of the day and she dozed, watched children's television and found it stupidly moving, then dozed again.

"Hello." Edward knocked at his own living-room door.

"You don't have to do that."

"Well. I don't feel comfortable. I don't know what I should do."

"Yeah." Maybe she should go. A sinking greyness in her limbs made her think she should go. But there was nowhere that would have her, or nowhere she could have.

"Do you . . . should you see a doctor?"

"No."

"You're sure?"

"It's happened before, I never went to the doctor then."

She heard Edward snap in a breath and force it out again.

"You're right about me. I will watch anything. You're quite right. But I do have to know it's not real. Jesus—real people frighten me. And if it was real pain . . . Helen, I grew up with that. My mother, I saw what Dad did to her. Or if I didn't, I heard it, I saw the marks. It was my fault then and it's mine again now. I was stupid to write to you."

"I didn't tell you not to. I didn't want to tell you not

to. You didn't do this; you weren't there." There was an uneasy pause that she wished she could leave unbroken. She couldn't. "You were stupid to write to me?"

"The way that I did." He moved to stand beside her chair, very still. "I had to write, but I shouldn't have done it that way."

"Don't let him make me angry with you. I don't want to be. You haven't done anything wrong." She leaned until her head could touch his arm. He let her be close, but didn't move closer. "Do you think we'll work, Edward. Do you think I can be here?"

"You need somewhere to stay and I need you with me."

He rubbed at her ear with his thumb and forefinger and she heard the shingly, seaside rush of sound close beside her eardrum. When she was a girl, she'd loved that noise. It was private, something no one else could ever listen to. For a moment he squeezed slightly and she caught the thrum of his blood, or her own.

"Helen, my work keeps me busy, but it's lonely when I stop. Especially now, when there's nothing else here. I would need you, even if I didn't . . . You know. If I didn't feel for you."

"Will we work, though?"

"I don't know." He tried that again, to make it seem hopeful. "I don't know. That's not something I'm professor of. But I think we'd be good." This time, he'd sounded mainly sad, so she kissed his hand.

Original Bliss

. . .

At first, Helen worried, imagining how they might be and what they might have to do to each other if they didn't take care, but the slow days they made together left her nothing but settled and calm.

She listened to Edward at night, his orderly pattern of preparations for his bed and sleep, and she rested in her room with his videos and books and was secure and undisturbed. She felt her conduct and presence here were justified, were all right, and her memory started her life with the day she stepped up from the underground at Gloucester Road. Glasgow wasn't hard to keep out of mind.

Helen came to believe she was good and could have good things. She didn't deserve them any less than other people she could think of. Edward was right, if she accepted all the facts about herself— the ugly and the clean—she understood who she was precisely, all the time. She hadn't done anything bad since she'd known her own nature and its controls. She had come to no harm and had been offered the chance to change away from what might be called sin.

There was always the possibility of sin with Edward. Undoubtedly what she felt for him was love, she admitted that, but her love need not be expressed in ways that were wrong and had to be paid for. She was learning how much salvation there was in the passage of time; it could re-form passion into friendship and let her live here, growing well and strong. Her sleep was obedient and prompt, her dreams unmemorable but happy, and if her God was watching she couldn't feel it and couldn't feel His loss.

Edward pursued his work, sometimes shouting in his study, emerging and pacing, then diving back again, but with an underlying air of fixed content. He began to make sentences involving the word *we* and talked about taking pains with his appearance because this made him feel clean and as if he were leading an upright life.

"Come and see my study."

Helen was newly back from buying milk, her face and hands anxious for the warmth of the flat. The warmth of home.

"It's nothing very interesting, but I thought you might like to see." He held the door for her, which was something he liked to do.

Only one wall was occupied with shelves. The other three were covered in photographs, drawings and picture postcards, fixed over each other like scales.

"They're lots of little slices through my head—the things I like to remember. I can focus on one picture and it will fire off through the whole day. It's a sort of music; so I can sit in here with an old friendship playing, or a nice day, or a good argument. I occasionally like to argue."

Helen was more interested in his dark, monstrous

desk and its huge computer. "I thought you didn't approve of them."

"Computers? They're things, instruments, nothing to approve or disapprove. I have a problem with the people who use them. The person who uses this one is me, so I like it fine. And it gets me into the Net. I love the Net. It carries proper information, facts with added emotional interference, irrelevancies, passions, general human subversiveness. People keep overrunning the machine and so it's full of Completed Facts and nobody in there has to forget *what* they are— human. They may forget *who* they are, but anyone can be lost in thought—thought is a very big place. Every day, I make a point of feeding the Net with new things conventional programming would not like: ethics, nonsense, morality."

"And I thought you were working in here."

"I do that, too. Honestly."

He looked so suddenly earnest, she had to rub his shoulder to make him smile.

"I know. You work hard, I'm sure."

"I'm sure also. Sadly, the Nobel people don't agree. Not this year."

"Oh, I'm sorry."

"I'm not. Not this year. I couldn't spare the time." He brushed her with a soft glance. "They'll have to give me one in the end. But back to morality . . ."

"Yes?" She noticed a beat between them, a flicker of something that quieted again.

"There is, of course, very human and understandable *im*morality on the Net. My printer could stay active, day and night, discharging uncontrolled configurations of anatomy. I could spend all day in here, having virtual sex. The screen's radiation makes you sterile but the text still makes you come. Neat, isn't it?" He didn't smile.

"And is that what you do?"

"No. I've never tried sex on the Internet. Not because I disapprove—"

"Obviously."

He pinned her with a tiny look. "Yes, quite obviously. I have never gone in there because I know I haven't got the strength of character to ever climb out again. I do harmless things in cyberspace: talk to colleagues, work. I spend my days at work. That's what I wanted to report. That all is safe and well in here."

"Um, good. Well done, then."

"Yes."

She felt very much as if she should shake his hand now, but didn't.

Edward appeared happy in a tentative way, grabbed a pencil from his desk and put it back down again. "Mm hm."

Helen's time gently expended itself in reading or walking, playing the tourist. At first she was unsettled by the air of satisfaction she noticed in so many of the people she passed in the street. Faces and bodies moved under a thin but unmistakable sheen of health. The shops that were closest to her calmly charged ridiculous prices and sold ridiculous foods while their staff seemed to appraise her and find her an introduction they did not wish to make. Locked gardens and high windows and craftsman-applied paintwork were all wadded in with a cool lead-and-smoke-flavoured air, only occasionally coloured by the stench of crumbled drains. But her new district's little brushes with squalor and the repetitive fuss of its prettiness gradually eased into normality. A person can grow used to anything. Helen learned that when she ceased to care about it, the city—like God—receded and let her be.

Sometimes she wished she had money to spend on Edward's house—to buy an ornament or picture that he wasn't expecting—but then, as he said, he didn't actually need any more than he had. Helen did no housework at all, not even the toasting of toast. Edward's cleaning lady looked after the house twice a week, taking care of everything but Edward's study and Helen's room—the two places she was asked not to disturb. Because she never saw where Helen slept, she made assumptions, but Edward and Helen did not. They made a point of dressing fully for breakfast and rarely kissed.

· · ·

"Forty-eight days."

Sometimes, he would pop through at supper-time and clear his head of work before he went to bed.

"That's a long time."

"Yeah. The fillings in my back teeth are fusing."

"What?"

He flopped into an armchair. She liked that none of the chairs belonged to anyone in the flat. They could both feel at ease sitting anywhere, although she did prefer the sofa, because it allowed her to stretch out and lie. She was getting lazy. Or comfortable. Sleeping and reading paperbacks and going out to eat—it made a comfortable life.

"No, only joking. Forty-eight days. Wouldn't have believed it."

"How do you feel."

"Great."

"And more generally? All this?"

"Great."

"Anything happening you don't like?"

"No."

"Anything not happening you would like?"

They both laughed instead of saying anything.

Their dinners with each other were different. She looked forward to them more.

"Well?"

"I don't know. Would it be enough, Edward?"

"For me? It would be perfectly enough for me. What about you? That's what I'm asking. If it's going to be . . . I don't want to do something wrong and I might because I don't know my way . . . around. You know I don't."

"It'll be, it'll be fine."

"Well, yes. I hope." He ran the curl of one finger down the slope of her cheek until the muscles in her back began to shudder. "Fine would be what I was aiming for. I haven't exactly studied the area properly. Not in a way that would help."

They were making Horlicks in the kitchen which seemed quite entertaining in a nicely pointless way and was also something for which they were both in the mood. She watched him stirring the milk and laughed.

"What? Am I a bad stirrer?" He looked worried happily, "What?" then just worried, "What?"

"I think . . . I'm not sure . . . what I think." She stood by him and squeezed his free hand around her wrist, her pulse. "Nerves."

"You feel frightened. I hope I don't—"

"You don't frighten me, I'm just nervous. Or . . ."

"What?" He danced his thumb down to the heart of her palm and left her with a broad need, drumming in the length of her arm while his eyes worried at hers. "What."

"It might be nerves and—heartbeat-raising things . . . those sort of things."

"Thank you for being so specific." Again his thumb grooved a charge into her veins.

"Expecting—you know."

"Expecting."

"Me expecting you."

"Ah, well, yes. That would do it. Quite possibly."

"That's the same speed, but not the same thing. And I'm . . . I don't know."

Edward turned up the gas and put her hand where she could reach her fingers in beneath his jaw so that she could understand the kind of time his blood was keeping. This meant she also touched his voice.

"After this, then. Shall we?"

"Yes, that would be—definitely, yes, fine. Hot milky drinks, though . . . they're meant to make you relax? Should we—"

"To make you sleep, actually." He watched her, peered clear inside her mind and tickled there. Her fingers felt him swallow once. "I should think we'll keep lively somehow."

"That's not unlikely, yes."

"Listen, it won't be anything we don't both agree."

"No." And she turned him to herself and held him because of wanting to and because she was scared. They both slipped inside a kiss, waited a slim moment while he caught her tongue between his teeth and then opened for her again, milk-sweet.

"We still have to do the Horlicks."

"Mm hm."

She felt him, hard in at her stomach and ribs—something to call down a murmur of sin.

"What should we do? If we're thinking of—"

"Moving on to other things? Well, I think it doesn't matter if the milk hasn't absolutely boiled." He lifted the pan experimentally, his unoccupied arm fast around her waist. "Do you understand about Horlicks?"

"As far as I can tell, you've been managing fine."

They didn't know where to start: which room would be best. The kitchen and the study were too unwelcoming, the bathroom wouldn't do, her bedroom was full of his past, his bedroom was his bedroom and would lead to things.

Living-room.

He drew the curtains, although the flat was far too

high for anybody to see in. You never could be too careful, though and, anyway, Helen had stayed nervous of that window, its hungry size, and Edward didn't want her to be nervous, not now.

"I'm okay."

"You're not worried?"

"I'm not worried."

"Because I'm right here . . . well, obviously—that's what this is all about—me being here with you. Helen, you'll have to forgive me if I sound . . . if I stop making sense during this. It's only that I'm getting preoccupied. With you. I want me to be with you." He adjusted his grip on her back. "Really, I think I should go and sit down over there.

"I'll be right here. Well . . . that's why we're both . . . It's only me, though. I won't change, because I want me to be with you."

But they still clung against each other, as if they were saying goodbye. Something was pouncing in her chest and panic was shining the length of her bones.

He perched on a chair and sat rubbing his jaw and looking beyond her shoulder. Helen had thought of sitting, but that didn't seem quite the right thing, so she waited as she was. She stood and braced herself against herself and the roiling need that was stroking the meat between her ribs and then dipping its head clear inside her, striking a light. It seemed superfluous that she should move in any visible way.

"Helen? Should I help?"

"No." He mustn't touch her, that would make things go wrong. "No. I'll start now."

She could hear him watching, while her fingers tried to unmuzzle her buttons, but she didn't look up. The best thing to imagine was maybe being in a changing-room at a shop. That would be the calmest option she could think of and he hadn't asked for a performance, only that she be undressed and that he could see.

The air shivered against her. Every slip of the cloth, each release, first followed her habits of motion and then altered beneath the press of observation.

She bent forward and carefully re-learned the weight and motion of her breasts. They were waking up. She stood to catch her breath, to be more displayed, and found that she could watch Edward watching, while her body met his eyes. He sipped in a breath. She stepped out from the last thing that hid what she was and gave him what she wanted, or at least what they'd agreed.

There was a certainty in her now, cold and unchangeable and planted in the opened flutter of blood at her heart. She was naked in the eyes of God. Raising her arms and setting her hands at the back of her head, she could feel His terror drumming under her womb.

Edward's face was lovely in an unfamiliar way and almost grave. His lips were parted, his gaze one unified, unfillable depth. Black. He blinked gently with a little frown. "Helen. You are beautiful."

His last word tingled against her stomach and she felt she might cry.

"You're gorgeous, that's what you are. Gorgeous." He murmured, making her strain to hear him, making her whole body listen in. "You needn't say, but I would like to know—maybe you could nod or shake your head—and tell me. Are you wet? For me?"

The question which makes its own answer. If she hadn't been, it would have made her; but she had been, so it made her more.

"Oh. That's nice. Thank you. I have to . . . I have to step outside for a moment, you know? Maybe, if you sat down. I'll just . . . be back soon." And he walked around the edges of the room and out of the door.

Without him there, she felt foolish, even slightly angry, but mainly alone. The leather of his armchair felt peculiar to her, cold and unpleasantly animal. She crossed her legs at the knee and stared at her dark reflection in the blank of Edward's television screen.

He came back and faltered to a stop when she faced him.

"I'm sorry. I didn't want to do something that would offend you." He studied her face. "Are you all right? I didn't want to leave you, I know it was the wrong thing to do."

"If you had to go . . ."

"Yes, I did." He sat again, not so far away that she didn't notice he smelled of soap. She was beginning to be cold.

"I know we said I wouldn't touch you and I do understand that. You are a person of principle and there are things you can't allow. I am not your . . . we're not . . . able to. But I did think—you're so far away like that. Don't you feel far away?"

"I suppose."

"Might I hold your hand?"

Helen let him have that: a small, formal contact they could have exchanged in the street. Either they'd already done far too much and were lost—might as well do anything now—or this was the way they'd control themselves and be reminded of how they could and could not proceed.

"I love you, Helen." Before she understood the words, hot shards of how they felt were carving through her, every way they could. "I do. I've thought a lot about it and I do. I don't want to frighten you or hurt you."

Helen had no reply, so she kneaded his hand.

"I thought I might . . . This is nothing you couldn't let me do, or I wouldn't suggest it, but you don't have to. I thought that now you'd done this for me, I could do something for you." He studied her patiently, giving her nowhere to hide. "And something for me, of course." He brought out a small pair of scissors from his pocket. "I would like to cut your hair. If I could."

"My hair?"

He let his gaze fall against her, so that she would feel it where he meant. "Not on your head." He nodded rather formally to the ache that was folding her back to her spine, made his proper introduction to her body. "There. I want to take care of you there. I don't have to, absolutely I don't have to, but you've let me see—and you are wonderful to see—if I trimmed, then I'd . . . see more. Will you? Let me? I promise I'll be careful. God, I'll be careful."

It was only when nothing was left to stop her but her conscience, that she found how small and liquid her conscience was. Edward pressed it and it poured away as she saw the metal shine of the scissors coming and liked to think how cool and odd they were bound to be.

A man should never touch another man's wife. The wife should not let him. If she moves she must not move to meet another man's touch, unless she has a failure of conscience and, even then, she has the moral law.

Without morality's prohibition to protect her, she will be stripped down to her soul and the empty fault inside it. She will feel the long, tight haul of the man being near her and the need swinging in her blood and she will move to it because she has no mind, no choice. The steel shock of twitching blades and the curiosity of fingers, they will be all she is.

Kneeling low, Edward snipped her in close to the

skin, taking pains at the slick of her lips. Helen watched her body being shorn back younger and opening under something hungry and new. When she came, Edward held his blades steady, but not far away and watched her with complete attention, watched right through her as if she were a wet perspective drawn on herself.

Then he talked to her: a nervy monologue that whispered in under his work. "If you're very still . . . really very still, that's it. Perfect. You are perfect. Completely. Just extremely nice."

She trusted him. No matter what he did, she would still trust him. No matter what he asked, she would allow and the thought of that covered her with a dull, sweet fear. She was finding out who she was. For months, her imagination had already known that he would be terribly steady and calm against her and terribly soft. She had faith in the way that he was and would be, and it would be so hard not to stay with him now, even though she was completely certain that he could do this and things like this any and every day. There would be no standing that. She would become the kind of woman who would want him to do everything they could think of and who would love it.

Edward had been speaking for a while without her listening, because she was only holding herself still, beneath the ebb and flurry of his breath.

"I can't look at you and think of the pictures. This

just isn't like them. They always end up the same way. I hate that. They always end up reaching inside women, reaching here." She rose a little to meet his description. "It's as if they were looking for something, just kind of searching around." His words landed, tepid against her thigh. "They always fumble at it like a jacket pocket, or something—the crack where they lost their spare change—and this isn't *like* that, this isn't *for* that." A thumb-stroke at her newer, sleeker self. "This is not a thing. This is you. But for the pictures, in they go—the same move for every possible occasion—checking for standard dimensions, getting a good grip."

Edward was keeping busy, fervent, while Helen felt herself slipping below his obsession.

"Then when I watch the women grab the guys' dicks and I look at their wrists, the action of their wrists, and they might as well be gutting fish—get the guy hard and toss him off with the minimum effort, the greatest efficiency. And you know this is something they've done a thousand times before, come after come after come. Repetition. When it's real it doesn't repeat. It's fresh. It's lovely. Beautiful."

He halted and the sudden lack of motion stung up through the muscle of her back. "This'll never be the same. I'll be learning you forever." And once again, the clipping: thorough and methodical to clear the way.

Edward didn't have to tell her, she quite understood; he was making her look like one of the women in his films, like what he must want, a body pared down to its entrances, a splayed personality. But even her disgust yawed and clamoured for more of him when he was finally done and drew his hands away, because inside herself she *was* like the women in his films.

Edward rested back on his heels, glanced at her with a type of helplessness and let his head drop. "I am going to stay here. You should get away to bed." He seemed unsure of where to put the scissors now. "Nothing happened that was bad, did it? And we agreed—all of it. I, um, know you've been very good to me already. But if you didn't mind, I would watch you walking out. If I could. The way you are now—to look at you this way would be wonderful."

He paused, folding his arms and possibly waiting for Helen to speak, even though he had removed her from any thought of words.

"Tell me if I've pleased you, Helen. You've pleased me. I mean, I've never been in a . . . similar position." He raised both hands to his mouth, breathed what he still had of her, and then bowed his head. "I'm very happy. I want you to be happy as well. You're better than anything else I know. Are you happy?"

"Yes."

Helen stooped extremely slowly to gather her clothes, precisely as he asked her to and then she left him.

Edward told her, "Thank you. Thank you very much."

In her room she climbed straight into bed, still stripped and still echoing with Edward, and she curled on her side and was private too late, her knees close up to her chest. She was not happy.

Helen did not expect to sleep, but down into unconsciousness she went, tiny cuts and strokes of horror mumbling at her as she fell.

A garden caught her; a warm, flat green place with soft trees and bushes and the high, close buzz of insects on every side. She was naked, but as soon as she noticed this, lizards began to drop from the undulating branches above her and flattened themselves across her skin. They covered her surprisingly well, but were chill to the touch and when she walked she could feel their claws tear at her minutely.

She passed an empty cave with a stone at its mouth and felt all the lizards raise their heads to look at it respectfully. While she brushed them back down into place, she caught sight of a bearded man, digging in one of the flower-beds with a narrow metal blade.

The gardener raised his hand in a sort of blessing. "Hello, Helen. Your lizards are doing well."

"Yes."

"Would you like to see my heart? It's sacred, you know."

"Yes, I would."

He opened his shirt firmly with a shower of loosened buttons and then let his arms fall aside to unveil a plump, glossy heart, winking and panting moistly through his parted ribs. Something glowed and wormed inside it like a lightbulb element.

"I could bless you with all of my heart."

"Could you?"

"Oh, yes. But underneath the lizards, there's nothing to you any more. A blessing won't do any good— you're past saving." He smiled beatifically and Helen tried to stop herself from staring at his chest wound while it trembled and sucked, inviting. She felt sure that if she could touch the heart it would forgive her and she would be saved.

The gardener stood, poetically casual with his arms still wide, as if he might be embracing something large she could not see. It was a simple thing to step forward while he eyed the wavering trees and to reach her hand inside him. The heart nuzzled her palm and let her touch the urgent ribbing of its veins. If she could hold it for a tiny while, then all would be eternally well, but as soon as she tried to grasp it, the heart ducked away from her and she knew this was in case her badness made it burst. Then slippery and hot, like the mouth of a meat-eating plant, the gardener's wound began to close and clasp around her in a massive, insistent bite. It shattered the bones in her wrist with a long, creaking snap, while the heart hid itself, now entirely beyond her reach.

The hot plumes of pain she dreamed lancing up her forearm, lingered momentarily as she woke into the silence of her room. Almost as soon as she remembered where and how she was, she realised her door had been opened and a figure was close to her bed. She lay, hypnotised by probabilities and the weight of their approach.

Edward.

Of course it was Edward, there was no one else for it to be. His soap, his toothpaste, his warm washed body; she could not help but breathe him in completely. Then a brief kiss, lightly clumsy, delivered above one eye and he padded away, sneaking the door shut behind him.

Helen lay on her back and peered up at nothing with her arms folded in across her breasts because that felt correct. This way she could check how solid she was, how much of her was really here. As she moved her muscle and her skin, the places where Edward had touched her felt different and light, but underneath was the dirt of her thinking. She would have left her room and gone to Edward and talked with him about what was on her mind, but she couldn't ask Edward for advice about leaving Edward.

That was why she had to go. She had to leave.

Helen was being emptied of all but the terrible

things that she wanted to do. She was fading away. Odd prayers had already begun to ambush her, full of insistent requests she'd never intended to make, prayers that knew she would be disappointed when a man left her bedside after only a kiss.

So in the morning she should go. She should make her usual breakfast and read the paper and have mar-malade and toast and do nothing to cause uneasiness or alarm. She should try to wonder aloud again how a man of such undoubted intelligence couldn't manage not to slop his saucer full of tea when he knew it made drips on the tablecloth eventually.

"I know, it's because I'm not awake."

His eyes were vaguely puzzled as he spoke. She had intended only to tease him, but had sounded bad-tempered instead.

When he finally left for his study she caught him by the arm and, at once, he leaned towards her without resistance, naturally letting her kiss him on the mouth as though this was a long-established part of their morning routine. His grin, the half-halt before he turned to the doorway and the nervous rub of his hand at his hair were the last things she saw of him, which made her glad because they were all very good to remember, very like him.

Helen left Edward's flat as she might have for a visit to the museum or the park and took herself to Victoria where the coaches are. With money that was Edward's, and for which she was sorry, she bought a ticket to Glasgow and then waited in the waiting area until it was time to go.

"Helen?" Mr. Brindle sounded—how did he sound? Not angry. Almost afraid.

"Yes, it's me. I'm coming back." And one more time, to convince herself, "I'm coming back."

"When?"

"Now." Silence washed back at her from the receiver. "I wanted to say . . . if you would let me come home, I would be there in half an hour."

"Let you?" His words were softening and softening, she could have mistaken him for someone else. "Let you? Come back. You really will? I thought . . . what I did . . . I thought. Thank God you're back."

"You don't believe in God."

"Thank God you're back."

The house made her ashamed. Mr. Brindle had kept the place neat, perhaps only a little more tired than when she left, but still, it compared badly with the

Kensington flat. Helen realised her tastes had been changed. She had come to expect the kind of simplicity expense can sometimes lend to things. Helen had stayed with someone who led the life of a wealthy man and who could afford to be careful of quality and design. Material things hadn't mattered to her before. They did now.

"I tried to be tidy."

Mr. Brindle escorted her doggedly upstairs past rooms she already found too familiar. Bathroom, box-room, bedroom. Outside the bedroom, Mr. Brindle stopped. He was keeping his distance—possibly finding her mildly repellent and she could understand that. Frowning towards her, he mashed his hands into the pockets of his jeans: very old jeans he wouldn't normally have worn around the house unless he was doing some type of dirty work. "Cleaning up. Dusting. It was like, it was a way of thinking of you." Everywhere smelt mildly of his sweat. "That thing that happened . . ."

Helen found she could meet his eyes quite firmly until his gaze withered away. He didn't like it when she watched him.

"That thing. I lost my temper. You know when I lose my temper . . . I don't mean it." She watched. "I won't do it again. You shouldn't have just gone, though. I worried . . . your sister, she didn't know . . . I won't do it again."

He nodded and retreated towards the head of the

stairs, wiping his hands down the front of his shirt and Helen knew she did not believe him. Even if he didn't think so, he would do it again.

Inside the bedroom, the mirror of the vanity unit blinked at her slyly and there was nothing she could touch or see that didn't seem ready to trip, to leap, to start up the process of making her pay for every piece of every wrong that she had done. She had come here to submit and Mr. Brindle would do God's will to her, even though he was an atheist.

There was, undoubtedly, the problem of her being a weak person in so many ways. She was susceptible to doubt and hesitation. When she opened her case to fetch out her bits and pieces, the atmosphere of that other place, of the flat, swam up to tug at her and make her current course of action seem confused and difficult to take. Almost all of her wanted to be in Kensington and maybe only lying on the sofa and feeling nice, at ease, and expecting that she would see someone she was very fond of quite soon, if he wasn't already there with her. She wanted to be comfortable. She had always wanted to be comfortable. Helen didn't like to be hurt. She enjoyed it when good things happened and she could show they pleased her.

When she'd been in that flat on her own, sometimes she'd put on the radio in the sitting-room and not exactly danced, but wriggled and bobbed, when she'd felt so inclined. Even if she hadn't been alone, it would have been okay that she'd done this and not something she needed to worry about. She had forgotten how much space in her mind the worry had to occupy, it was already burrowing and smothering every image she was holding inside when she wanted the freedom to remember incidents and people she cared about.

"Helen." Mr. Brindle was shouting from downstairs, although moderately loud speech would have been perfectly audible. "You going to be up there all night? You're home now. Okay?"

She abandoned her case on the bed, still full.

Mr. Brindle was calm when she joined him in the dimness of the living-room. He sat in his usual chair, watching a documentary about something to do with crime, and was not especially fatter or thinner than before, but made out of something very minorly different. His flesh seemed more porous and less convincing.

"Sit down. You travel far? Tired?" He didn't look at her.

"Not really. No."

"Fine. You'll sleep in the spare room. Sheets and stuff are out." He didn't look at her at all.

"Yes."

For an hour, the television jabbered recklessly between them. They did not speak again, or draw the curtains, or turn on the lights. Helen watched the room coagulate around her under shrapnel bursts of light.

Whatever he was planning to do with her would clearly involve a wait. Helen knew that tomorrow Mr. Brindle might consult with the men he worked beside, or ask opinions at his pub on what he should do and how he should feel about his wife. The influence of like minds could very often make him angry with her, even if she had not.

Helen, because she could be so easily frightened, had hoped there would be no wait and no opportunity for her to break and run away to softer things again. Still, nothing was wasted in God's economy and the time she was being offered could be put to use. She might be able to prepare herself.

But this particular part of her waiting—waiting in the fluctuating dark with the television noise and no hope of distraction from the man and the name and the telephone number she could not think about—it was no longer bearable. "You know—"

"What?" Mr. Brindle must have been pausing all that time, ready for when she would speak.

"I just thought I would go up now."

"Well I won't be long behind you." He made a small, breathy laugh, either out of nervousness or disgust. "Not long now."

"Fine. Good night."

She didn't attempt to kiss him because that would have given him the chance to turn his head away.

.   .   .

Mr. Brindle had done well for her in the boxroom. The old wardrobe had been emptied and then refilled with a tangled heap which was all of her clothes. A small stack of paint tins occupied the corner furthest from the unmade bed. The carpet had been hoovered and the walls were penitentially bare. He had left her sheets and blankets and a small electric fire to annoy the damp. When she switched it on, it clicked and rang and produced a fine, acid burning of dust.

All right, God. I'm here. What do you want me to do? Be my shepherd, be my father, let me know what I should do.

She stopped, didn't open her eyes, but called a halt to herself. Her breathing raced towards a strange anticipation. She listened and could hear the jump of her heart. Careful, now, be careful—this could be nothing, wishful thinking and nothing more.

Helen was kneeling, because a person at prayer is intended to kneel, as a signal of humility and respect. Body kneeling, hands folded, eyes shut—all of her curled and closed to keep out this world and permit its better replacement to enter in. To enter in. For years she had knelt and protected the vacuum that she was, her absence of the convincing and the convinced.

She needed to be very careful and still. As she might be if she hoped to touch a nervous bird.

She should consider the degrees of pain. She should recall the degrees of pain that emptied prayer had caused her over time. To accept her loss of faith and fall silent in defeat had been a relief, but then a burden. God knew, she'd tried to be rid of it. God knew where that had got her, too.

And then a brief stab of inspection dropped through her. The house seemed to lurch around an axis and return almost before she could think. Quiet again. But an ordered stillness, packed and immanent, laid itself down on the backs of her legs like sweat, near as live hands cupping her face.

All right, God. I'm here.

While she opened her mouth to breathe, an inward rush took her and squeezed to her spine. This time the sensation dissipated as gradually as smoke in her veins.

Helen opened her eyes and the boxroom was unchanged. She couldn't think what she'd expected.

A sign.

Stupid.

Might as well hope He might leave His umbrella behind.

And it wasn't even that He'd been here. Not that. Only that He was close.

Close. The kind of word to make a person cry without knowing it. Close. A movement of hope behind glass.

Father, I'm here and I don't know what to do.

After that the speed of everything went wrong. Helen performed what tasks she could remember were called for about the house, even performed them over again, and was still left surrounded by abandoned hours. Walking out to the park, the shops, up and down the stairs and corridors, made no impact on her energy or pace. Every morning Mr. Brindle left her and every evening he returned and she had no sure way of judging what had passed between those two directions— it could have been a minute, it could have been a week.

Maybe not really a week, she didn't think they'd last a week before it happened.

"Cunt."

Wednesday evening, meal over and at every point satisfactory, but then she'd tried to bring him a coffee in the sitting-room and dropped the cup. Her hand had forgotten itself. Mr. Brindle heard the impact of the china and the liquid as they came apart, stood and watched for a still moment as the dark, wet heat sank into his rug.

Then he stepped forward and slapped her. "Cunt." Slapped her in the face where it would show because he wasn't being careful any more.

Nothing followed, but in Mr. Brindle's eyes, Helen saw the sharp start of intent, before he could pack it down again. Naturally, she was afraid, but she tried her hardest to accept that her fear had meaning; it was part of her Process. It would make her soft and open, the way she had to be.

Because each night she would kneel and be raced

towards the increasingly completed fact of God. Larger than understanding, deeper than death and time, He would hood down over the house like snow, patient and immeasurable.

Father.

So the time drops by you like blood then eddies with uncertainty and after days of waiting you still wait, discovering the way this feels cannot be unbearable because you bear it. You are not yet fully prepared, you have to remember that. This final interval is here to make you ready and complete.

Praying becomes all you do, it ribbons around you while you move in the world and tells your life out and up to that Watching, that anatomising Stare. You step from daily fear to fear until the sun sets and the house begins to move in time with the nasty itch in your husband's hands. Not long now.

Friday night. Twenty-two hours gone out of the twenty-four and you're kneeling, again kneeling, in the room he's given you and you hear him on the staircase and in the corridor and this time, like every other time, something important tears up under your ribs when he passes your door without coming in.

Your husband doesn't come in, but you know that

tonight isn't over because you've changed; there's nothing left of you to say; you've let God see it all. Not that you could have believed He didn't fully know about every layer of tissue He's asked you to peel away. The point is, you had to tell Him and He had to hear. This was your part of the Process and your Father who art in Heaven, but who is also much nearer and much more terrible than that; He will forgive you now.

Forgiveness. Feel it pick you back down to the child, take you off your hinges and clean you to the bone. He's here, your Father who is tender like a furnace and who will hold you for eternity, if you would only ask and He can make you ask. He can make you go through fear into somewhere else entirely.

It is something like half-past ten when you go to Mr. Brindle's room, the bedroom you at one time shared. You are aware of a lightness in your hands and limbs, the tiny noise of your feet and the press of black air against your flesh, your cleaned and uncovered self. Second-hand illumination seeps out around the door-frame. To be at this point already, so quickly, you hadn't expected that.

Turn the handle, open the door, absurdly prepared for it to be locked or for the bogey man ghost to leap out and take you at once. Walk in, gently, because you are standing at the edge of nothing and you don't want to slip. Mr. Brindle is sitting up in bed, staring at a paperback which you have the time to recognise as one of the detective stories that he likes. Crime: nothing else caught his interest as intensely, and what does that say about why he married you?

Magically slowly, he lifts his head.

He does not make a sound.

There is a slither of confusion in his eyes and he glances away but has to, in the end, come back to you. Your body is balanced, naked, and breathes fast from the top of its ribcage, as anxious as any discovered animal, and Mr. Brindle's mouth thins to a stroke while he reaches your eyes and you offer look for look and beat him. Then you feel the precise ignition of his anger, just as he helps himself to the rest of you in a long, falling glance and sees what you need him to see.

You are not as he remembers, not quite. He moves his head a scrap to the left and examines again. Not the same. He is finding out what Edward has done to you and what you wanted Edward to do to you and enjoyed, and you can think of Edward now, very clearly and with love. There is nothing to stop you thinking whatever you like.

Now Mr. Brindle understands. You have been sheared in tight to yourself, to your nothing-but-sex, and each of the questions he chose not to ask you and the hardest assumptions he most liked to make are proving inadequate.

You are turning and walking back out at an even pace when you hear Mr. Brindle rip himself up from the bed.

The knowledge of him behind you and on his way

scalds from the back of your neck to your heels, but you will not run or even rush. There is a bang of complaint as the door cracks round against the wall and shudders in again. Mr. Brindle beats it away. He's in the corridor.

You have nearly reached the boxroom. He is closing on you very fast and now makes a sound which swipes you off balance as if it were a blow. You have never heard a noise like this from a person before: a high, long howling that jars with every impact of his running feet.

You make the room, halt and enjoy for an instant the impression of being safe, of an objective successfully reached. Then Mr. Brindle hits you, the whole of him hits you, drives the use out of your lungs, and you fall with one hand reaching down ahead of you to shield your face.

"You didn't die."

"Yes, I did. I felt it."

"No. You didn't die."

Helen opened her eyes and saw the unfocused shine of a metal counter while somebody's hand adjusted the bend of her knee. She knew that she was dead and they were laying her up on one of those special tables they had for autopsies. It was very unfair to be doing all this while her mind was still inside her body.

"Leave me alone."

"We will in a while."

A different hand drove a spark of hurt so hard into the bone of her leg that it exploded her understanding along with the table and the room.

So Helen was cut loose and floated for a time she did eventually calculate but never quite believed. Small pieces of reality would swim out to meet her and then sink from sight. She became accustomed to the notion that her body was being kept somewhere, lying in uncomfortable clothes inside a bed. The rest of her was mainly unwilling to be anywhere, having an idea that any kind of definition would involve it in the guaranteed discovery of pain.

Her hair was stiff and sour-smelling when Helen moved her head and at night people took her blood pressure all the time when she was so tired that the grip of the cuff on her arm made her weep. She was unconvincingly thirsty and could not remember if she had ever been given a drink.

Sometimes the gardener seemed to come and talk to her with his heart—the heart liked her now, it was warm and insistent against her fingertips.

"Helen?"

"Yes."

"What were you going to die for?"

"You."

"I never asked you to."

"I guessed."

"Helen, did you think if you were meant to die, we would even consult you?" He smiled when she couldn't answer him. "Have you touched my heart?"

"Yes."

"Has it touched you back?"

"Yes."

"Then go away and be satisfied."

A woman arrived to polish the floor under all of the beds and Helen woke for long enough to take the scream of machinery back down into her sleep.

Beyond every dream or darkness, Helen watched and watched a sort of dance where Mr. Brindle twirled her body so that it banged and cracked and splashes of light appeared with colours in time to his beat. As their finale, she would spin against the wardrobe and tug it down to cover her and keep her safe, or to let its weight finish the death Mr. Brindle had started for her, she couldn't be sure.

"So you don't remember."

Helen frowned, cautious. Without any warning, she was conscious and apparently taking part in a conversation.

"You don't remember anything after that?"

She was staring up at a policewoman with a soft expression and no hat. The policewoman frowned so Helen said something which felt correct.

"No. No, I can't remember anything."

"He telephoned."

"Who? Did somebody call me?" Hope suddenly thumped at her, but she explained to herself that Edward wouldn't call—she had left him and not said why, not said anything because she had to come to Glasgow to make things right.

The policewoman, rather than giving an answer, was shifting her weight and glancing across Helen's bed to a policeman. He pursed his lips and dropped his head forward in a way that might have meant he was nodding consent, if you knew him very well. He was trying not to move or be distracting; supportive but invisible, that's what he was aiming for, Helen could tell.

The policewoman gave a nod of her own and began, "Mrs. Brindle." She cleared her throat. "No, nobody called you. Your husband called us. That night, or at least, very early that morning, I think it was . . ."

"Two fifteen." If you want to know the time, even an invisible policeman can't help but tell.

"Two fifteen. He called us to, to turn himself in. He thought he'd killed you. You were under the wardrobe when we came."

"I didn't die."

The policeman gave his sleepy nod again and very quickly patted her hand, as if he was scared he might catch himself doing it. "No. That's right."

Another small cough and the policewoman continued, "When we arrived, Mr. Brindle was relatively lucid and rational." This had the sound of something that was already firmly written down. "He let us in and told us where you were. An ambulance was called. He expressed, I'm afraid, no relief when he was told you were alive. At this point he informed officers present that he had taken a large number of paracetamol tablets some considerable time before."

"A very unpleasant way to die." The policeman offered, almost consolingly.

"Yes. That's . . . Yes. Any treatment offered after internal damage has been done can only be a sort of management. They made him as comfortable as possible. This must all be very shocking. I am sorry. His brother has identified the body that—"

"Won't be necessary. You won't have to." Again the pat at her hand.

They seemed very gentle, these people from the police, and anxious to only ask and say what was absolutely needful. She had the impression they might have sat by her bed before, or perhaps they had met when she was under the wardrobe and not thinking but still listening—perhaps the sound of them was familiar. She would have liked to tell them how she felt. Certainly, they seemed keen to know her feelings and ready to help if she was unhappy. But she wasn't unhappy—she was awake and she was alive and those were two such remarkable things, she had no room for any more.

The policeman gave her a quiet smile as he and his companion finally stood. "You'll be numb, that's what it is. You'll be numb—these things, it's how it happens." He nodded a great deal while he said this, but watched her as if she were a problem that might not be solved conveniently. Both the police then left her alone to work out the finer details of herself, because they had everything they needed and, even though they were obviously pleasant, they had other duties which, most likely, called.

Helen lay and watched the light fall impeccably from the neon strips above the ward and thought that moving her eyes and paying attention and saying sentences and all the time being careful to make no savage or even tiny movements of her head was far too much to be doing at the one time. A rest was required.

Something very easily accomplished. In years to come, she could see herself emerging as a champion sleeper: started late in life, but now an eager narcoleptic, a woman who liked to be able to leave any situation simply by strongly favouring the interior of her own mind, safe behind darkened eyes. Night, night.

When her new dream was steady and she could stand and look about her, she knew at once where she was: in the kitchen of Mr. Brindle's house.

"What are you doing here? You're upstairs, dead."

Mr. Brindle was sitting on the floor in his dressing gown. He turned his head up to glare at her and she saw dark matter begin to purl from one of his ears. He scratched at the side of his face in irritation, but seemed otherwise quite normal, perhaps overly pale. His voice hadn't changed, it still had enough edge to make her seem shorter and weaker than she was. "Go back upstairs."

"I'm not dead."

He smiled slyly, sensing a trick ahead. "You will be." A sudden cough distracted him. His lips were turning blue. "You'll die and be nothing, like everyone else in the end." He wiped at the sides of his neck and examined the rusty stains across his fingers. A great deal of him was leaking away as Helen watched.

"Today I am not dead. You didn't kill me. You couldn't. And I let you try."

"All right, then, I killed myself. I know I killed someone." Another cough. "So it was me. I'm dead. What'll you do about it?"

"There's nothing I can do."

"You aren't going to pray for me? Like a good Christian should?" A laugh bubbled in his chest but couldn't emerge.

"Oh, I'll pray for you. I can pray now—about anything. I'll pray because I'm able and because it will help me. And because I know you'd hate me to."

He smiled, a sheen of blood dulling his teeth. "Cunt."

After that the dream clouded over and she sculled out into something smooth and aimless that allowed her to feel rested and content, even when they came to take her blood pressure again.

Mr. Brindle was dead and she was not. Sometimes God was really very obviously good. You didn't have to understand it, you just had to accept—God was good. He did well. He gave her things she was not expecting.

Like the sight of an anxiously tall figure walking softly down the ward, his concentration on the floor. Not a dream and not a mirage: a man with an extremely severe haircut, wearing a long grey overcoat and a very red scarf and putting his hands in his pockets and taking them out again, as though they could not be comfortable except in motion. The scarf made her close her eyes for a moment, it was so bright.

"Helen. Helen, are you awake?"

"I'm awake. I've got a terrible headache, though."

"I should think you do—you have a fractured skull."

She blinked up to see Edward folding his arms and tilting himself away from the rest of the ward while he tried to pull in a smooth breath. The muscles in his jaw ticked with an effort at control, but still he started to cry.

"Shit."

Helen tried to reach and touch him and her attempt sent the walls and ceiling spiralling. She lay back and let the vertigo subside. "I've got the headache—you don't have to cry."

He fumbled for a chair and lifted it close to her bed, all the while repeating quietly, "Shit, shit, shit," and rubbing the heel of his hand across his eyes. "Why the hell did you go back there?" He sat. "Was it me?"

"No."

Taking her wrist, "Was it me?" and then letting her slowly move her hand to set its fingers round his thumb and grip. "Did I upset you?"

"No. I had to get back here and sort things out."

"Sort things out? He could have killed you. You

must have known that. Couldn't you even have phoned?"

"You would have come and got me. You would have done the right thing, but it would have been too soon." Edward didn't speak and pulled his hand away from her.

Helen thought of God. It was important He was here for this. If God was God, of course, He would be in each of her bruises and her water jug and anything she could think to name—but she needed His help to say what she must.

As soon as she opened her attention, Something monumental began to pour in. A sense of humour must obviously be amongst the everything that God had—for years she'd needed to hear from Him just a little and now He was determined to be deafening.

"Edward? I can't turn my head to look at you, I get so dizzy. You'll have to speak to me. Please. I am sorry I hurt you, I didn't want to."

"No, you only wanted to hurt yourself. What were you thinking of?" His words choking out, breaking. "Jesus, I come up here and I find the house empty and then the neighbours say what happened, only they don't really know what happened . . . I thought I'd go mad. Helen, I could have got you, I could have been here in time. He never would have hurt you if I'd been here."

"I know."

"I would have stopped him."

"I didn't die."

"You could have."

"But I didn't. I got through. I was taken through. I mean, I'm *alive*, Edward. I believe in Something—or Something believes in me. And I believe in me and I can do any and every living thing a living person does. I am alive."

He drew his chair in with a scrape that made her smart. The smell of his hair, his sadness, his skin, was an astonishment as he leaned in to set his voice neat beside her face.

"Helen, I intended to come here and be . . . acceptable. I couldn't be where I should have been to help you and I know that what I did made you go away." She tried moving her head to disagree and he kissed the rise of her cheek. "I want to tell you all the things that a good man would, all the right things, but you know I'm not good."

"Tell me, anyway."

"I can't. I can only say what I want and that's frankly quite inappropriate."

"Tell me, anyway."

"Helen, I want you to be alive with me—the whole completed fact of you with me. I want to do that. God, I got so lonely down there. Because I can't do what I used to any more—the films, the magazines—and I'm telling you, I gave up fighting it and tried and it didn't even matter, because I couldn't do it, couldn't even begin. I just missed you. There's nothing I can do about missing you. I haven't got anything when you're not there and I don't know what to do with me on my own, with myself."

She felt him press his forehead into her pillow and lifted her hand to touch his neck and then the tight trim of his hair.

"Helen, I should go. They said I wasn't to upset you."

"You're not. Tell me something."

"What?"

"How do I look?"

He lifted his head and blinked at her. "How do you look?"

"Yes. Tell me."

"Um." He began a kind of frown. "Just now?"

"Just now."

She heard him pull up a breath to speak with and then stop. Then he breathed again. "Do I have to get this right? Helen? I mean help me, I don't know what you're asking. I love you. Can I say I love you? I love you."

She felt that. It washed along, snug under her skin, slow and heavy and more than enough to stir up the pain in her bones. She held him by the wrist with as much strength as she had. "Mr. Brindle never told me how I looked. So I want to know. And I love you."

"You . . . ?"

"Love you. How do I look?"

"Well, you're—really?"

"Yes, how do I look?"

"Um, you look lovely. That bastard—he didn't stop you being lovely. Your nose is a bit . . . He broke it." His hand smoothed light on her forehead, catching a hair back into place. "I would have killed him. Murder has no possible justification, I believe that absolutely, but I would have killed him if he hadn't killed himself—I would have. Sorry."

She felt his face grazing above her, breathing her in.

"Helen? That thing they've given you to wear, I wouldn't—I don't think it's very nice."

"I'm a mess."

"You're a lovely mess." He surprised himself with a laugh that ended dangerously close to something else.

"Oh, well, I've never been a lovely mess before."

"It won't happen again."

"I've been a *mess* . . ."

"No. You're still doing better than me. Listen, you may not be able to see this, but I am in no way at what we might laughingly call my best. Shaving this morning, I don't know, I can't have been thinking—I look as though I've tried to cut my head off. Blood everywhere."

"Don't let the nurses see, they'll keep you in."

"I wouldn't mind staying." He paused to let her think about that. "Helen, could I bring you a different nightdress tomorrow? If I came tomorrow . . . I could come tomorrow. I live here. I have a flat, I'm renting a flat, that seemed to be the thing . . . I mean, would that be useful? Something more comfortable for you to wear?"

"That would be good of you. Thank you. I'm a si—"

"I know what size you are, Helen. I know exactly what size you are."

A porter wheelchaired her out of the hospital because her walking was strong, but her balance much weaker, and she represented a risk of accident to herself. Edward loped, or occasionally had to trot beside her. She was being discharged to his flat and his care which made this feel like a fixed prescription, as well as a choice on her part. There was a good solidity about the plans for her immediate future. Edward had admitted his qualifications in matters of the brain and friendship and the proper authorities had accepted him as a person who was fit to have charge of her. In spite of, or perhaps because of his doctorates, the ward sister had given him a checklist of contra-indications for cases of head injury.

GROWING DROWSINESS OR CONFUSION

WEAKNESS OF AN ARM OR LEG

VOMITING

LEAKAGE FROM THE EAR OR NOSE

SEVERE HEADACHE

"I've had a headache for a week." Sitting in a rented flat and drinking badly-made tea and thinking she is more fond of her city now than she has ever been and that the autumn sky through the window is of the very best colour in a blue eye and good enough to break your heart.

"For a week."

Edward is busy being pleased. Helen's sister bought clothes and cried and looked at him as if he might very well be a monster and he was still pleased. Whatever he does or does not do, he cannot help being pleased. At the moment he is smiling at Helen in a way that means he will be slightly deaf, because he is not listening a bit.

"Headache. Me."

Now he is concerned, but also pleased. "Not a severe one."

"How do you know?"

"I'm a doctor."

"You're a professor."

"I had to be a doctor first. Does your head seriously hurt?"

"No, doctor. I just wish it didn't spin."

"I know, that'll wear off, though. Your balance is out of whack."

"You don't say."

"Oh, but I do, I heard me." And he takes her temperature the way he is meant to at regular intervals, especially at night.

Helen thinks of him at regular intervals, especially at night, and she grows more well. She walks without help, she can bear to read print, they take her stitches out. For the very last time, she talks to the police and all they discuss is no more of her concern. There will be an inquest and she will get through it because Edward will be there.

One evening she sits in the best of their flat's remarkably purple armchairs and eats a hot meal with Edward. The people that Edward telephoned have cooked it, but he puts it on the plate.

"So it's edible, at least."

He starts their washing-up and Helen follows him in to make a pot of tea. They both enjoy their tea. When she fits herself behind him as he works at the sink, they both sway slightly under the impact of what they are because they haven't touched this way since Kensington. She slips her hands in round his waist until they meet above the buckle of his belt. He leans in to her, only lightly and she can feel all of him live, "Are you sure?" and each of his syllables rubbing and snuggling in. "We don't need to hurry."

"What have I got here?"

"Me."

"Mm?"

"Edward E. Gluck. The E is for Eric. I don't want to rush you."

"I know."

"But I will have to in a minute, if you don't stop. I'm only flesh and blood, after all."

"I know. That's what I want."

"Is it?"

"Yes. It is."

Which takes them to her room and to the drawing of her curtains and to a kiss which is so interesting they are unable to move on for quite a while.

A person should not undress another person while that person is undressing them.

"I'm sorry, it's because of the dark—if you could do that button." Edward does have extremely large hands, which are not always un-clumsy.

Helen is finding it difficult to co-ordinate speaking with the everything else that is happening everywhere. "Different, isn't it?"

"What?"

"Clothes. Going from the outside in. Someone else."

"Mm hm. Different and much better. Oh, God. No, I'll do that, because it's . . . Okay, you do it, then. But—"

"Ow."

"Sorry, I did say . . ."

They stand and clasp each other woodenly and

Helen thinks they are afraid of breaking or of the roaring of their skin or of the fact that they have exactly what they want, that they are holding it.

She walks him to the bed and they cover each other up, carefully and entirely, and begin the gentle, strenuous fight to cling and be still and kiss and move and touch every place when there are acres of places, all moving and turning and wanting to be touched. Edward's skin, she could never have fully imagined how completely satisfactory Edward's skin would be. And he has a good weight, the right weight, something she can move to take.

"Can I?"

"I wish you would, yes."

A stutter of hands and there he is, the lovely man. In.

"Jesus that's—" The other stutter, the big stutter. "Oh, Helen. Oh, I'm sorry."

"No, stay there."

"But I've—"

"I know." She can feel the twitch of him, the slight withdrawal. "Stay there, though, I like you there. And we have ages, we have all night, we have years. I'm taking it as a compliment."

"I was hoping it would be." He coughs, relaxes, sinks on to her. "Not exactly the demon lover when it comes to flesh and blood."

"From what I've read, I shouldn't worry, we'll be fine."

"From what you've read?"

"Self-help books, they cover everything. I've gone through most of them."

"And you've read about this."

"About all kinds of things."

"You're as bad as me." She feels him twitch again.

"I came across sexual information in the course of my general reading."

"Really." Twitch. He is smiling in both possible places.

"Yes, really, and sometimes I wanted to read about men. I wanted to like them, because often they seemed such a good idea and not the way I'd been told, or the way that I'd found them to be. I mean, they go wrong; any kind of person could go wrong, I understood that, but then I'd see a man walking or tying his laces, or something, queuing in a shop and he'd be so lovely and clear . . . He'd be the way a woman couldn't. I'm a woman and men are made to be particularly not like me. That is such a good thing. Like men swallowing . . ."

"Swallowing."

"Yes. Have you ever watched a man swallow—absolutely nothing but that? It's incredible. You've all got that high adam's apple and it moves so fantastically well—like it's happy and buoyant and vulnerable and working just the way that it should be—and the jaw's got a proper edge and there's that bit of friction. With men you get friction. They can really be a quality design."

"I'm glad you approve."

She rests her mouth near his throat and he swallows for her. "Mm hm, that's it."

"Well, I'm a man."

"I know that."

"I swallow like a man."

"But you swallow like you, too. And you have your kind of man's chest. When you stand up, it's at that right kind of an angle, that clear line—no breasts."

"What about my angle now?"

Helen licks his neck and closes her eyes while his body gives a gentle jump and hers answers it. "It's a good angle."

"Anything else, while you're making a list?"

Her hand makes a slow reach down to where it wants and he shivers up for a moment to let it through so it can hold him.

"These would be on the list. These are the best. Very nearly the best."

"You be careful with them, then."

"They're gorgeous, they feel gorgeous."

She explores while Edward stretches full awake. "Oh dear."

"What?"

"You didn't read that in a self-improvement book. Unless it was a very good one. Oh, dear."

"If you don't like it, I can stop."

"Don't you dare. You have no idea of how many nights, of how long I've been thinking of your hand doing that, and of me being here and inside you and doing this with you, and this."

They begin doing this, and this, Edward talking them through.

"Oh, God . . .

"That's nice . . .

"I think . . .

"If we . . .

"Make it slow . . .

"This will . . .

"Turn out . . .

"Fine.

"Oh, yes.

"We're Fine.

"Love you."

"I love you," and so she does.

Her thinking is beginning to steam over, but Helen knows precisely who she loves and precisely Who has let her love him.

"That's it."

"No, that's it."

"Oh, yes, so it is."

They're almost away now, almost one and the same thing and not a thought between them except for, "Edward?"

"Hm?"

"You have really large feet."

"Feet?"

"Mm."

"Now she tells me."

"You do."

"I'm very tall." Bright at her ear, breath and sound and Edward being pleased to sound mildly offended. "Didn't have big feet—I'd fall over. We wouldn't want that."

"No, we wouldn't want that."

And, having nothing more to say, Helen lets herself be. She is here and with Edward as he folds in around her and she around him and they are one completed motion under God the Patient, Jealous Lover: the Jealous, Patient Love.